Honesty & Integrity

DISCLAIMER

"This is a work of fiction. The events portrayed in this work are fictional. Any resemblance to characters living or dead or situations is purely coincidental. While some settings for this work are real, they are used for dramatic effect; however, the events do not depict actual events."

Visit www.booksurge.com to order additional copies.

LARRY D. CAMPBELL

HONESTY &
INTEGRITY

2007

Honesty & Integrity

TABLE OF CONTENTS

In Loving Memory Of My First Wife Barbara Campbell. She Was The Driving Force In Our Marriage And She Passed That Fortitude On To Our Daughter.

CHAPTER ONE
The Players

Mike Zipp jumped when his cell phone rang. Being a Las Vegas cop for three years you think he would have gotten use to bells and alarms going off. He was riding with his best friend and partner Jackson Thomas. They had been close since they were twelve years old, when they met at the Boys Club in Erie, Pa. They graduated together and both went on to play football at UNLV, taking advantage of the scholarships they both received. Mike had been a fullback and Jackson was a tight end.

The ringing or I should say singing phone meant that a friend either male or female was probably in trouble. When Mike answered he heard Tom's excited voice hollering into his ear to get his ass over to the bar as a fight was about to break out. Tommy Thompson owned a great local's bar that a lot of the cops hung out at when off duty. Tom was smart enough not to call headquarters as that would result in a black mark against his business and too many of them would mean he owned a trouble bar and he might get closed up. Half the time it was the off duty cops causing the trouble anyway.

Mike and Jackson were both big strapping young men. Mike was 6'1" and 220 lbs. Jackson was taller at 6'4" and 240 lbs. They both were into weight lifting, boxing and karate. Not exactly Kung Fu masters but they knew enough to handle almost any situation.

Jackson Thomas always said that Mike Zipp was the toughest white boy he ever knew. Mike grew up on the lower east side of Erie and learned to fight at the East Side Federation Club. Jackson was from the projects and both used athletics to get them out of Erie, Pa.

When they walked into Tom's Looney Tune Café the first thing they noticed was none of the six or eight people involved were off duty policemen. In fact they didn't see any fellow officers or friendly faces at all. Declaring themselves as "Police" didn't help much; in fact it seemed to make matters worse. They were soon fighting for all they were worth. Two of the combatants must have snuck out or were hiding and the other six were either out cold or slumped on tables or in chairs. Each thought the other must have really kicked some butt because the entire melee lasted about a minute or so. Mike knew he only threw three or four punches and Jackson was thinking likewise. They threw out the troublemakers after giving them a stern warning not to ever come back again or they would be arrested. They then high-fived each other, teased Tom for his lack of help and bad back and left with the promise of free drinks when they got off duty that night.

Walking into the Looney Tune at 12:20AM they looked more like strutting peacocks. Tom gave them both a couple Miller-Lites and told them to come to the back room. Tom said, "I want you two young studs to look at something." Tom had security cameras throughout the bar like every other establishment in Vegas. Tom turned on the monitor and you could clearly make out the two studs with "POLICE" on the back of their patrol shirts wading in among the chaos. Tom pointed to the right of the screen and said, "You see this guy here drinking a beer and minding his own business?" Jackson replied, "That old bald guy?" Tom answered, "Yea, and watch the old guy move." One of the thugs bumped into "pops" and he turned around with a smile. The punk said something and swung a haymaker at the old guy. The old guy caught his fist in mid swing, put his arm behind his back and threw him out the door. On the way back to his stool another punch was thrown at him and he simply ducked under the punch, grabbed him by the back of his neck and belt and launched the second tough guy out the door. As soon as he got back to where he was sitting he did a quick turn to his left and side stepped in front of two individuals that were about to hit Jackson from behind, one had a cue stick. "Pops" dropped them both with two quick jabs you could barely see. He then sat back down, picked up his beer and starting watching the TV again.

Tom looked at Mike and Jackson with their mouths open and that peacock draining look on their faces. When they could finally speak they wanted to know if Tom knew who their unexpected helper was. Tom said that he had been coming in almost every night for about a week. He said that he had an unbelievable sense of humor and always had the bar in stitches. He left tonight about an hour before you guys got here with another young attractive female and that's the third different one that he knew about. Tom says, "I think he's from back east, maybe Philly, and everyone calls him "LC". I'd say that's his initials or a nickname."

Two nights later and a rare Saturday off, Mike and Jackson walked into the Looney Tune Café, both with a gorgeous showgirl under their arm. They heard a roar of laughter coming from the end of the bar where most of the patrons had gathered. After getting their drinks from Tom and teasing him about not sending down the cute mini skirted barmaid, Tom said, "It's too hard to get her away from LC. But she'll have her stiffest competition from Kassaundra." Kassaundra was a beautiful light skinned black female cop that both Mike and Jackson had been hitting on since her first day on the job. They could barely see LC past the crowd but they could see a very sexily dressed and smiling Kassaundra under his arm and she had both of hers wrapped around him.

The first thing they were both impressed with, besides his obvious charm and success with the female gender, was how well he was put together. He was mostly bald with light brown hair graying at the temples. Dancing blue eyes that highlighted a pleasant face that glowed with integrity and character made up his persona. They figured he was about 5'11" with a thick neck and his arms were bigger and more defined than both of theirs. Mike and Jackson hadn't noticed on the monitor during the fight how well LC was built. Maybe the monitor wasn't that clear or maybe he had on a baggy shirt that night but now in the light and only about 10' away they could make out a not too small waist and a thick chiseled chest. He was standing with a beer in his hand, wildly gesturing and talking trash with a getting wetter by the second Kassaundra sitting on the bar stool with her arms around his hips.

Jackson motioned to the barmaid and she grudgingly came down the bar and he ordered drinks for Mike, himself and their dates. He also instructed her to get LC and Kassaundra whatever they wanted. He also told her to tell LC they wanted to talk to him whenever he could get away from his admirers. The barmaid made a remark under her breath about "that bitch he's with" and began to fill their order. When she returned she asked Jackson if he wanted to put that on his tab and said LC would be down in a minute.

A short time later LC walked down to meet the two young patrolmen and their dates, and a clinging Kassaundra was with him. She proudly introduced LC to her two coworkers and they in turn introduced him to the showgirls. LC shook their hands in a true friendly manner and kissed both girls on the cheek. Both men saw the immediate glee and interest from their dates at this simple affectionate gesture. Both men also felt an immediate liking for this man. He definitely had a way about him. He was charismatic, charming, funny and friendly, but most of all he was a legitimately nice person.

Jackson began and Mike joined in by thanking LC for his help two nights previous. LC just chuckled and replied that it wasn't fair for them to have all the fun. Mike told him that they had watched the video from the security camera and wanted to know how he came to move like that. The two Vegas cops could handle themselves and have seen many of their fellow officers "get tough" when they had to, but these were men in their 20's and 30's. LC looked to be in his early to mid 40's but he may be 10 years older than that. Although nothing in his physical appearance or his sharp wit or apparent intelligence gave away his true age, it was more of his confidence and the way he carried himself that left you to believe he was older than he appeared.

Out of the blue Jackson's blonde date blurted out what they all wanted to know, "How old are you and where do you come from?" Without a pause LC replied that he was 58 years old. "I'm too old for one of you but just right for both of you." He quipped. Both girls giggled and all four of them believed it. Then he added, "I don't judge age by how many breaths you have taken but how many times your breath has been taken away." The young men knew they could learn a lot from LC. He then told them that he was from Philadelphia and was a retired supervisor from the Graterford Prison. Every cop in the nation knew of Graterford Prison and there was no doubt as to where he learned his survival techniques. LC denied that and said he got fast and learned to duck when he was married to his first wife. "Toughest broad I ever met, and the hottest," he quickly added with a reminiscent smile.

LC had been coming to Vegas for years and decided that when he retired he was going to see what it was like to live here. He said he had won about 50% of the times he came out here on vacation. He played Blackjack mostly but knew all the casino games well. He mostly liked the atmosphere and the people.

After finding out that LC had brought his golf clubs along, Mike and Jackson got LC's cell phone number and promised to call him with a tee time. LC said he gambled a lot better than he golfed.

Six rounds of golf, a couple hundred beers, a thousand laughs and two weeks later the guys were getting along famously. Probably infamously would be closer to the truth. The skirt chasing and the number of seductions would make an old sailor blush.

LC told them that he was at Graterford for 25 years. He started there at 31 years of age and worked his way up the ladder. Much to their surprise, especially Mike's, LC had played fullback for a semi-pro football team. The team disbanded when he was 31 and he knew some large guards that played that also worked at Graterford and that's how he started his corrections career.

CHAPTER 2
The Problem

Mike and Jackson walked in to the Precinct on Thursday morning a little fuzzy in the head but still laughing at the antics LC was pulling off the night before. Sgt. Jones hollered over their loud guffaws that Captain Cimini wanted to see them both as soon as roll call was over. They both looked at each other with that "What did we do now, look."

Twenty minutes later the two men walked in to the Captain's office looking like two well screwed sheep. Captain Cimini was a good man and a fair man, but he could look over his glasses at you and make you feel like a puckered up mouse. The Captain didn't go for all that formality stuff with salutes and shit, he simply said, "Park your asses." Mike and Jackson quickly sat down as the Captain closed the door and the blinds.

Sitting down heavily and of course peering over his glasses the Captain started with, "I'll get right to the point. I understand you guys know a person by the name of Lassiter Carson." Jackson and Mike looked at each other and both shook their heads and said, "No." Captain Cimini then added most people call him LC. The Captain failed to see the humor in the question as both men cracked up over learning of LC's real name. They had never asked.

A half hour later the Captain came back into his office. He had to rush to the men's room as he had laughed so hard over the related LC stories the men told him that he almost pissed himself. As he calmed down he began to get very serious. He told Mike and Jackson that he had two first cousins that worked in corrections. One in Graterford and the other in Harrisburg, Pa. They knew the name of Lassiter Carson very well. "They say he's a friggin' legend." The gang leaders at Graterford passed the word around that if anyone messed with or tried to harm LC in anyway that they would pay the ultimate price. That is if there was anything left of them after LC got done with them. They say he never punched anyone but he had given a mighty slap to many. The reason he was so well respected is the fact that he never wrote anyone up. He solved the problem on a one to one basis. If he was accosted by a new inmate that didn't know any better he simply put them on the ground and took control of the troublemaker and the situation. If they persisted because of stupidity or youth or pride, they would get "the slap." That was always the total finality of the incident. The fact that he never wrote them up on institutional charges meant that the inmates didn't lose any of their privileges like phone time, rec time or visits from family or friends. That's why he was "the bomb."

"Now what I am about to tell you stays in this room," the Captain said leaning forward in his chair and lowering his voice to not much more than a whisper. "This is between the three of us, and two more that only I know and can trust and that is it. There is some illegal shit going on in this precinct with some unknown officers. I'll tell you more as to exactly what it is as I find out what all it is and who I can trust and who I cannot." Jackson leaned forward about 6" from the Captain's face and asked him how did he know that he could trust him and Mike.

Captain Cimini said that he had a few reasons. "The main reason was that jewelry heist at Balley's. The manager was positive 18 pieces were stolen, you guys found 22 at the perps apartment all in the same little velvet bag. No one else but you two and the thief knew the exact amount and he might not have actually counted them. If you would have kept one each and handed in 20 you would have looked good."

Mike asked, "How do you know there weren't 24? I thought about having my nipples pierced." Captain Cimini said, "You have been hanging around LC too much."

"Another reason, Mike you were born in Punxsutawney, Pa." "You're right Boss, but I don't know the groundhog," Mike quipped. "Well, LC was born in Dubois about 15 miles away, and I think there is some solid people stock in that area."

Jackson asks, "Tell me Mikey, you see a lot of black folk in that area?" Mike replies jokingly, "Not since we traded our slaves for chickens." Mike and the Captain were both laughing as Jackson started choking Mike and making remarks like, "Yo sho was a good masta to work fo boss but now I gots to kill yo, sos yo don't finds out about me and Missy Zipp."

CHAPTER 3
The Plan

Mike asks, "Tell me Cap, What's LC got to do with our problem?" Captain Cimini leans forward again and reveals his idea to solve the problem.

"If we tried to get a new cop in here maybe from Internal Affairs, undercover or whatever, he may get hurt or worse. I don't know how far up the ladder or how deep this all goes. So, instead of a quiet, sneaky undercover type that would stand out like a red mini skirted whore in church, I'm thinking just the opposite. A boisterous, funny, likeable kind of lout that draws attention to himself would never be suspected of being on the inside. Someone enjoying life and going through it with a smile, and in this case a plan, is just what we need."

Jackson says, "Well, there is no doubt LC could handle the assignment and he certainly fits that job description, but how do we talk him into it and how would we pay him for his services?" Cimini replies, "Ten percent of all drug money can be used for baiting and buying and at last count there was $140,000 back there. I don't know if drugs are the problem in this case but let me worry about how to channel it. You guys set me up with a meeting where we can talk freely." Mike asks, "How's your golf game?"

On the way out to the golf course the following Sunday Captain Cimini related to the guys something he had heard from his first cousin at Graterford. His cousin was a sergeant there, the same supervisory job LC had when he retired. Apparently LC had some run ins with the Warden and the Deputy Warden in charge of security. The state spent $25 million on an expansion plan at the prison to prevent over crowding. When it was completed there were flaws that LC and other guards saw and reported to upper management. LC had found a way, that with some outside help, an inmate could break out in 15 minutes or less. He personally took the news to the Deputy Warden of Security. His response was, "Don't tell anyone!" After another incident when upper management lied to his face LC was fit to be tied. But the real slap in the chops came when LC put in his bid for a Captain's position. Everyone figured LC was a shoo-in because he knew every aspect of the job so well and had trained the majority of the younger officers. Out of the blue the Warden announced that the candidate must have a college degree. LC had been to college but was forced to drop out because of the hardship to his family.

The four men had teed off after the proper introductions and LC was playing very well until the third hole when the Captain brought up the subject of his ex-bosses. Mike and Jackson saw a side of LC that they didn't think existed. He always seemed so cool and laid back, so in control of himself, but a dark and scary side of quiet anger began to immerge in their new friend. No man in his right mind would want to be on this black road to hell. Mike, Jackson and the Captain all saw it in his eyes and Cimini felt unnerved for bringing up the subject.

For at least a half hour LC went into a narrative of how worthless and inept his ex-bosses were. He stated, "What pisses me off the most is that these people act so high and mighty and a little known fact is that the Warden verbally abused his wife and the Deputy Warden cheated on his."

Then he started to smile. "I got even at my retirement dinner. At the end of my short speech I stated that a college degree was definitely something to be proud of, but I don't recall any college or university offering courses in honesty and integrity, and if certain individuals would have come and asked me, I would have been glad to tutor them in those fields." LC laughed loudly and as quickly as it came his anger had left him. He sank a twenty-two foot putt. "The whole audience stood, applauded and cheered, everyone except the two assholes." And he chuckled again.

CHAPTER 4
The Proposal

The Captain lost 6 balls on the first 5 holes and was down $2.50. Being notoriously cheap with his own money Mike and Jackson knew it wouldn't be long until he quit or at least brought up his proposal. "Lassiter," the Captain surprised everyone with his approach, "I have something to discuss with you that stays with us. It is something very secretive and possibly very dangerous as well. I would like you to hear me out, mull it over for a couple of days and get back to me through these golf pros here."

"What's on your mind, Gaylord?" Mike and Jackson damned near pissed themselves hearing LC use the Captain's first name like he did and them not knowing how he knew it.

"I've got some underhanded shit going on in my wheelhouse. I'm not sure who all is involved or how high up it goes. I am almost positive that dumb and dumber here are not mixed up in it." He nodded in the direction of the two clowns still laughing heartily.

Jackson slams a 300 yard plus drive down the middle and Mike reacting to the Captain's jest says, "That's a goodin' Bubba!"

"What I would like LC is to have you use your charm and ability to make friends easily and see if you can find out some info for me. I think someone quiet and sneaky would be suspected right away but someone boisterous and open like you would never be expected to be on the inside." The

Captain continued, "I can't guarantee you a definite amount of payment for your services but I will get you paid a decent sum of money."

"Damn Captain, if you are paying me out of your pocket I won't be able to buy a sno-cone." Mike and Jackson had to look away and hide their smiles and stifle their laughter. Apparently going over his head the Captain said, "No, it'll come from some unused drug money we have and anymore that you might come up with if it involves that but I don't think it does."

LC then asked what tipped him off to the fact that something was dirty at all? Jackson listened intently as Mike putted for a birdie because they wanted to know that answer also. The Captain stated that he had a very trusted confidante that worked at city hall in the recorder of deeds department. He said, "I know how much money these guys are paid. Jackson and Mike here spend all they earn on whores and booze and have nothing to show for it." Mike chirps in, "What about our big, happy smiles?" Ignoring Mike the Captain continues, "Some of their fellow officers who make even less money than these two yahoos live in $300,000 homes or have two smaller ones. They drive expensive cars, wear Rolex watches and other jewelry. Last year two of the guys and their wives went to Paris for two weeks and that ain't cheap. And their wives don't even work.

"The only thing I insist on LC is that you go to my personal doctor and get cleared. I'll have you fill out insurance papers, both life and hospitalization, and I'll keep them in my desk drawer at home. You know just in case something happens."

LC said he wouldn't have to think it over. It wasn't about the money, he was just getting a little bored partying every night and chasing young attractive women. Of course he said that with his tongue in his cheek.

CHAPTER 5
The Physical

Captain Cimini contacted his personal physician and life long friend Dr. Kebort. He confided just a little bit of the plan to him and instructed him to put LC through the paces. The complete physical was to include a fitness test also.

The next afternoon the Doctor called the Captain on his personal cell phone as planned. The Captain asked him how the physical went and how much he owed him, claiming poverty as always. Dr. Kebort replied, much to the Captain's relief, that he owed him nothing. "That was the shortest physical I have ever performed, even on youngsters. As soon as he entered the waiting room I heard Susan the receptionist screaming his name as she ran around the counter to hug him. Apparently they had dated a few times. She abruptly informed me that he was very healthy and had the stamina of a man half his age. That was more information than I wanted to know. I also figured that there was no reason to check his prostate. After I checked his vital signs and his lungs I asked him if he thought he would be able to do 20 or 25 push ups. He said he would try. He got down on the floor with his feet against the wall and proceeded to perform 25 push ups. At that point I decided the physical was over and useless. He did the 25 push ups one handed." The Doctor also related to the Captain that the ten minutes or so he waited in the waiting room he had the staff and all his patients laughing hysterically.

CHAPTER 6
The Prognosis

Captain Cimini and LC met at a little diner west of Henderson, NV. LC told him that he was certain that Kassaundra was either involved or at least knew of the wrong doings. He informed her of the shitty circumstances in which he left the corrections field. He said he told her that he was basically not a vengeful man but if he ever had a chance to take down his ex-bosses he would bury them. There were also two Philly detectives that were in on a scheme to demoralize and humiliate him. Between the four of them they manufactured evidence that might have even gotten him indicted and sent to prison. They said they had a witness that placed him at a house of a known criminal and their investigation showed that he was part of the illegal doings. "Being street smart myself and their stupidity saved me," LC added. "The time that I was supposedly seen there I was at work training 10 or 12 new correctional candidates."

Kassaundra told him that she had grown up in Philadelphia and lived near Temple University. She had been poor all her life and she had witnessed too many stabbings and shootings. She came out to Vegas with two men she had just met. She said she was willing to do anything to get out of that hell hole and she humbly stated that is exactly what she did. One of the men has a brother on the Vegas Police Force and he talked her in to applying. "It was that or prostitution," she told me. "She would be rich right now if she chose the latter," LC added. "I'm kind of glad she didn't make that choice, I like that girl." Captain Cimini spoke up, "she's a damn fine cop and I'm glad she didn't choose to whore but I sure hope you're wrong about her possible involvement, I would hate to take her down." Then LC added, "Apparently she still had trouble making ends meet until about 6 months ago. She said she finally got smart or maybe stupid, but now at least she has some easy money coming in."

"You know Cap," LC went on, "I think there is some kind of a Vegas/Philly link. Kassaundra lead me to believe that me being from Philly meant something more than just coincidence. When I find out more I'll call Jackson or Mike to set up another meeting. Right now, it's more of a feeling than an actual fact."

LC paused, "I'm supposed to go to a party with her this Saturday night at some cop's house." "Did she mention his name," Cimini asked. LC replied, "I think she said his name was Sanders, Dave Sanders." The Captain looked up quickly, "Sanders owns that $300,000 home I told you about. When Dave and his beautiful wife first came out here and he got a job on the force they had this old Pontiac. My son had one just like it and he sold them the tires and other parts off his when he bought his new car. His wife was working at a jewelry store. I think she went to school for that kind of work back East. I never did know exactly where they are from. I ran into her about a year ago at the Vegas Mall and I asked her if she was working at one of the jewelry stores there. She told me she had quit about three months earlier. I watched her walk away. She has a fine booty and she was dressed very chic. I also remember she got in and drove away in a new Caddy. I thought maybe she received an inheritance or something."

"If I were you LC, I'd play down your friendship with Mike and Jackson. Call it instinct or intuition but you might find out more if you let on that you're not happy with them." LC said, "I'm not, the last time we golfed they took me for $20.00 each. Do me a favor Cap, tell them that if I approach one or both of them in public and start an argument or fight to go along with it. I don't want them to back down too easily but I don't want my ass kicked either. They fight very well. Explain to them the reasoning behind it also."

"Another thing," LC's brow furloughed as he leaned over with a serious look on his face, "How far are you prepared to go with this?" Cimini replied, "As far as we have to. Right now it might only be a white collar crime. I mean I don't believe anyone is being physically harmed, but greed has a nasty face and I know from experience that when push comes to shove, people get hurt. That's why I would like to pull the plug on this as soon as you can obtain enough evidence before someone gets hurt or worse. I know you can handle yourself but I don't want to see you get in harm's way. Get me some proof, get in and get out. If you were injured in anyway it would be on my conscious alone."

"You know Captain Cimini, you are just the sweetest guy," LC blew him a kiss and chuckled.

CHAPTER 7
The Party

Pulling into the long circular driveway LC mentioned under his breath to Kassaundra something about Vegas cops making a pretty good wage. Then he added, "Either that or his wife is an entertainer and makes the big bucks." He of course was fishing for information but it was an innocent enough statement. Immediately Kassaundra replied that his wife didn't need to work. "Well, not much anyway. She is attractive enough to be one though." LC stated that he would have the prettiest girl at this party. Kassaundra blushed, thanked him with a quick kiss just as the valet attendants open their doors.

Being open and brash got him through life and LC wasn't about to change now. It would be too out of character for him. As soon as Kassaundra introduced LC to the host he remarked how beautiful his house was. Dave Sanders thanked him politely. LC then stated in a louder than usual voice, "Wow, the graft out here must be pretty good to get a castle like this!" That was a typical remark for LC to make but he made it for a totally different reason. He wanted to see how many guests just laughed it off or how many felt shame, embarrassment or uneasiness. There was a slight lull in the action, but very slight, and then everyone laughed. LC estimated that there were about 30 guests at the party, those that he could see anyway. At least 10 were cops, some were showgirls and some were wives or girlfriends. He could not remember a more handsome gathering of individuals. Kassaundra was throwing names at him left and right and remembering names was never his strong point. He was however, very good at remembering faces. None of the cops looked familiar, but a few guys grossly over dressed for this climate with their arms around some of the showgirls did. He was sure he didn't meet anyone at the party since he had been in Vegas. During normal conversation while mingling about LC mentioned that he had met a few Vegas policemen at the Looney Tune Café. Kassaundra verified that and stated that she had met LC there.

Some of the girls announced that they were going swimming in the pool. As many of them took their tops off unashamedly LC blurted out, "Man, I love Vegas." Most of the guys were heading down to the billiards room and Dave Sanders nodded his head toward LC as a gesture for him to come also. Kassaundra put her hand over LC's eyes and said, "Get going, you'll see much more later on."

LC was about half way down the stairs behind his host. He couldn't resist giving Kassaundra a quick but passionate kiss and a pat on her fine butt. Dave Sanders turned right at the bottom of the stairs leading into the billiards room. LC could see the immediate waving of his arms in the mirrored wall at the bottom. He also saw something very shiny being quickly covered up and carried away from the pool table. Of course LC acted as if he had seen nothing. Actually, that was easy because he was genuinely impressed with the lay out of the room. It was very tastefully decorated. A thick deep navy blue carpet covered the floor and that matched the cloth on the pool table. Everything else was white and mirrored.

LC had that same feeling in his gut that he had when he was being interviewed for his prison job 26 years earlier. It was also the feeling he got when the Warden and Deputy Warden called him in to ask him questions about bullshit that never happened. He refused to be intimidated then and he refused to be intimidated now. The men mostly just stood around with drinks or cue sticks in their hands. He noticed Beverly Sanders, Dave's wife, for the first time standing behind the bar mixing drinks. He didn't remember seeing her there when he first entered the room. Either she was down behind the bar perhaps looking for a bottle of Grey Goose Vodka or she came in a secret door that he couldn't see. One thing he did see was that she was stunning.

LC had a vague idea that he had seen her before. He thought he must be getting old if he had trouble remembering where or when he met this rare beauty. The three older guys in the dark 3 piece suits were standing up at the end of the bar. They were watching him intently. Beverly poured a fancy blended drink into each of their tall glasses. She poured the exact amount in each one right to the top without a drop left over. He was impressed with her expertise. She leaned over and kissed the oldest gentleman next to her and said to him, "I'm so glad you could make it out here for our party this weekend Daddy, I missed you."

A slap in the face or a kick in the groin could not have brought back the memories as quickly as that small gesture of affection. Although, he was sure he had been in total control of his emotions and facial expressions he could not have been 100% certain. He momentarily thought about what Captain Cimini said about getting in and getting out as fast as possible. LC now knew it would not be that simple. He immediately made up his mind, if asked about his recollections he would be totally honest about them, or almost anyway.

Twenty or so years ago he had met Angelo VanDini after being arrested in a fancy Philly suburb. He could not remember the crime or crimes that he had committed that got him into Graterford Prison. LC did remember that he had to strip search him as a new inmate and that he had a small weenie. He couldn't help but chuckle to himself. He also remembered about 15 years later he was at a ritzy Philly nightclub drinking shots of Tequila to celebrate his good friend Sgt. Sawtelle's birthday. They both were drooling over the gorgeous barmaid that was new but showed definite promise. She had opened LC's beer perfectly and she had a little twitch to her hitch when she popped off the bottle cap. Sawtelle informed LC that night that she was Angelo VanDini's daughter.

Beverly asked, "And what would you like to drink, Sugar." That's the same thing she asked me eight or nine years ago LC thought to himself. "Beer would be fine and thank you," he replied. Pop! Off came the top, and there was that same little hip flip.

A large burly man with a big grin introduced himself as Manny Ruiz. As he and LC shook hands Manny informed him that he was a Vegas cop in his 5th year on the force. He then asked LC where he was from. "Philadelphia," LC replied loudly, and half the men in the room turned suddenly in his direction and he noticed Manny's smile fading from his face. "I retired from Graterford Prison a little over a year ago." LC was a little surprised that the fact that he was from Philly would cause such a stir. He thought sure Kassaundra would have informed them of that little tidbit and they would have taken that info in stride.

VanDini asked him how long he had worked at the prison and LC told him, he then asked LC what all did he do there. LC replied that he had worked at just about every duty station over his 25 year career. "The last 10 years I was a Supervisor so of course I did as little as possible. I got paid for making decisions and what I had learned over the years." VanDini unashamedly stated that he spent 8 years in Graterford on a bum rap. He also said that he didn't remember him but Graterford was a big place. LC said, "You must have behaved yourself while you were in there because I normally had to deal with the assholes and troublemakers." Then he asked, "Do you remember how long ago and what time of day you came in?" VanDini replied, "1979 in the late afternoon, why?" LC replied that back then he was already in his thirties but being newly hired he was still considered a rookie. "I probably strip searched you when you first came in. I got stuck with that job a lot in those early days. I looked up more assholes than a Proctologist."

LC turned quickly to Beverly and apologized for his poor choice of words but she was laughing just as hard as everyone else. She pooh-poohed his efforts and stated that she has heard it all. She then asked LC if he had ever been in the Velvet Pickle. She said she worked there as a barmaid while going to school to learn the Jeweler's trade. He replied that he had been in there a few times but that it was a little too rich for his pocket. He stated that he didn't remember her but that he definitely should have remembered a lovely girl like her. He then added, "But then again my brain has been fried for a few years now."

CHAPTER 8
The Pool

Someone said we probably should join the girls, and LC was all for that. The change of atmosphere would give him time to think and the change of scenery would certainly be refreshing.

Most of the girls now were topless as was Kassaundra. She more than held her own with the showgirls. She came over where LC was gawking, kissed him and said that she had missed him. He would genuinely hate to have to take her down if she was indeed guilty of something. He felt an attachment for her. It was his damn pompous idea of honesty and integrity that would make it right in his mind but it would still bother him. He decided he would cross that bridge when he came to it. She was exactly half his age.

Kassaundra asked him what he was thinking about. LC answered truthfully, "You." She said, "You better be, a couple girls have already inquired about you." LC replied, "They must be the smarter ones." A short jab to his ribs stifled his laughter.

She then looked into his eyes and a strange look came over her face. She was about to say something but decided not to. LC asked, "What is it?" She replied that it was nothing and this was definitely not the time or the place to discuss it. LC stated, "Always keep this in mind, you can tell me anything, I have heard it all and I have seen it all." Kassaundra purred,

"Thank you." LC decided that he would bend his rules for her. He would learn to live with it.

The party by the pool went on all night. To his dismay he only saw Beverly Sanders once or twice. Also to his dismay she kept all her clothes on. He figured she was behaving herself because her father was there.

LC was trying to figure out exactly where her father and his two associates fit into this scheme of events. His intuitions told him that it was more than just an out of town party for them. He figured they must still live in Philly because Vegas people wouldn't dress like that, especially at a pool party with the temperature still in the 80's.

The restrooms were in a cabana type bungalow right there near the pool. A ladies room and a separate one for the men, although they had those cutesy circles with crosses and arrows that LC could never get straight on the doors. He could hold back the call of nature for a long time but after 10 beers it was getting close to wiz time. An idea came over him and he approached his host. "Dave," LC said, "This is kind of embarrassing, I love that Tex-Mex food you served but it runs right through me. If I use the men's room here the entire area will be off limits for awhile." Dave chuckled and said, "No problem I know exactly where you're coming from. I'm the same way. Go into the house, instead of going right down the stairs to the billiard room, walk another 5 feet and turn left up the stairs, the bathroom is straight at the top. It has a great exhaust fan in there." LC bowed his head and replied, "Bless you my son."

LC looked around quickly for Kassaundra but didn't see her. He put his hand on his stomach to fake a gas pain and off he went. He glanced down the stairs of the billiard room. The main lights were off but he could see a faint light coming from the bar area in the mirrors. He turned up the stairs and found the bathroom. LC turned on the light and fan and proceeded to drain the main vein. He put thumper away, his nickname for his penis, and quietly walked out. He left the light and fan on, didn't flush, cringed at not washing his hands and closed the door. He then snuck back down the stairs. He could hear the raucous laughter coming from the pool area. He proceeded quietly down the stairs to the billiard room. Near the bottom staring again at the reflection of the light by the bar he could make out Beverly's head. She appeared to be sitting down in a small room behind the bar. She was holding something dark up by her one eye and she was totally engrossed in something before her.

A chill ran down his spine as he realized someone was coming. He had nowhere to go but down. He got on his hands and knees and crawled under the pool table. He hoped whoever was coming would not turn on the main overhead light. They didn't and he was glad the carpet was dark as he blended in the shadows.

His last recollection of Beverly before dropping to his knees was the jeweler's eye piece she was intently looking through. Kassaundra's familiar voice began talking to Beverly. He could make that out but only bits and pieces of what they were saying. The muffled tones they were using combined with the clamor from the pool area made it almost impossible to figure out the topic of conversation. LC didn't dare to try and get any closer. In fact a quick and quiet retreat was in order.

LC made it to the top of the stairs much to his relief. As he started to go up the ones leading to the bathroom he saw a figure above him almost at the top. He watched the person in the three piece suit hesitate, place his ear against the bathroom door for two or three seconds, he then turned right and disappeared. Without delaying for a second, LC started up again. His heart was pounding like a freight train and it was exhilarating. He could get use to this James Bond bullshit. He opened and closed the door behind him like a church mouse, flushed the toilet and started washing his hands. He started to breathe a sigh of relief when the door burst open.

She was pretty, topless, well endowed and looked great in her tiny red thong underwear. She was also very drunk and sick. Being the consummate gentleman LC was holding her hair back as she vomited profusely in the toilet bowl. LC had a big smirk on his face. From what he just got away with, what he just found out and from this little hottie with her butt in the air, this should be a good day.

Kassaundra failed to see the humor in the situation. She was standing in the door way and she was not smiling.

CHAPTER 9
The Passion

On the way home to Kassaundra's apartment LC refused to argue with her. He understood how it must have looked to her when she entered the bathroom at the Sander's house. He explained exactly what took place, omitting his wanderings. What he really couldn't figure out was why she was so outraged. They hadn't discussed placing any restraints on each other. Their relationship was basically still in the dating stage. He had been out with her four times including the night she introduced him to Mike and Jackson. They had pawed and clawed each other but had gone all the way on only one occasion. She had gotten drunk the first three times and LC had a holistic approach to being intimate with a woman the first time if they were inebriated. Kassaundra had asked him about his reasoning why he was completely opposite of most men when it came to the seduction of a woman in her cups.

Like most of LC's ideals of life his answer was both moral and hilarious. He had explained to her, "You know when men go out sniffing and chasing women and at the end of the night when their judgment is clouded with booze, they'll pick up fat chicks." Kassaundra, with a quizzical look on her face stammered out, "Yeah." LC continued, "Well, I don't want to be the fat chick." She remembered at the time he told her that she didn't understand the meaning of his morality but he had explained further. "If you woke up the next morning with a hangover and was dismayed with yourself for getting drunk and having sex with Lassiter Carson, that would be a kick in the butt to my machismo." She decided at that exact time that she wanted to see much more of this man. She had never met anyone like LC before. She doubted if she would ever meet anyone like him again.

Kassaundra got very quiet for a few moments. LC was concerned, he liked her a great deal and did not want their relationship to end, such as it was. She was quiet because she knew that she had over reacted. This was the most honest and decent man she had ever known and she didn't want her petty jealousy to screw things up between them. She had to believe him. She honestly did not think he would hit on and grope someone that was both drunk and sick. In the beginning she had taken the initiative when they were alone during their intimate moments, so why would he be any different now. The girl was very pretty and built very nice but so was she.

LC shut off the motor and looked at Kassaundra. She had a tear in her eye and he began to apologize for upsetting her. She stopped him in mid sentence with the most passionate kiss she could muster. That kiss alone would have killed a lesser man. LC thought, "Wow!" Not a bad way to die."

Fortunately the sun would not be coming up for another half hour or so. One man watering his lawn down the street got an eyeful as LC and Kassaundra taking off and carrying most of their clothes managed to get just inside her door. Two hours later they finally left the kitchen and made it to the bedroom where they continued their lovemaking. They both wanted more of each other.

Kassaundra opened her eyes at 3:15 Sunday afternoon. She had no idea what time she finally fell asleep from exhaustion. She had no idea what time LC had left. She rolled over on her side as she decided she needed at least another three hours of blissful rest. She laid there for ten minutes and got up. Her mind was spinning too much to doze back off. She knew she was falling in love with LC. She knew she did not want to get him mixed up in her mess or for him to ever find out. She would have to make some sacrifices but it could not and would not be Lassiter Carson.

CHAPTER 10
The Pilgrimage

L C did not get much information from the conversation between Kassaundra and Beverly Sanders while hiding under the pool table the night before. There was one thing he remembered that meant very little at the time but it was something he decided to incorporate in his plan. Kassaundra had asked Beverly how long her father would be staying in Vegas. Beverly had replied that they were flying out Monday at 3:00 from McCarran Airport. LC thought that her reference to "they" meant Anjelo and his two cronies would all be leaving.

LC called Kassaundra about 8:00 Sunday night and expressed his surprise that she was out of bed already. He stated that he would have to do a little better the next time. She replied, "If you perform any better you will have to call 911 for me."

He informed her that he had received a telegram from his lawyer back East. "That's the first telegram I've ever gotten in my life. I don't have my E-mail set up out here yet," LC said. He hated to lie to her, he hated to lie period, but this was underhanded work he was doing and it had draw backs. He could reason with his decision. He made up a story about his IRA pension trust fund thingy that needed his personal attention. He was going to try and get a flight out on Monday to Philly and would probably be back by the weekend.

Kassaundra said she would miss him and anxiously await his return. He was glad she made that statement as he would miss her also. He also noticed that she failed to mention that Angelo and his friends were heading to the same destination.

LC managed to contact Jackson and told him to inform the Captain of his pilgrimage to Philly. He also told Jackson that he missed his and Mike's company. "We'll have to go out and really tie one on when this is over," LC added.

Jackson agreed and told him they were aware of what Cimini had told them about what to do if a phony argument started up among them. "Mike and I have been wearing our Kevlar vests when we go out off duty. We don't want you breaking our ribs you big ass," Jackson chucked and they both laughed out loud.

"Hey LC," Angelo hollered out while standing in line at the check in counter. All three men had big, warm smiles on their faces. He summoned LC to join them and asked what he was doing at the airport. LC fed him the same bullshit line he had told Kassaundra. Angelo asked him where he was sitting and LC informed him that he wasn't sure if he could even get a ticket yet. Angelo took charge as always and purchased an open end first class round trip ticket for him. He produced the other half of their first class tickets he had purchased in Philly. When the girl said that there were first class tickets available but the seat beside them was not, Angelo handed her a crisp $50 bill and that took care of that small problem. LC protested but Angelo would not hear of any of it. "I've never flown first class in my life and won't know how to act up there." LC said with an appreciative smile.

The four men were sitting comfortably in their seats with a drink in their hands and the plane hadn't left the gate yet. LC thought Angelo might be a crook but he certainly was cordial.

He surmised Angelo might have an ulterior motive behind his generosity. His two comrades, Tony and Tony were very friendly to him also.

About an hour into the flight Angelo asked LC about his date the past Saturday. "That girl is definitely hot." Then he asked, "What's her name again?" He was playing dumb and LC knew it but that was fine with him. "Kassaundra Johnson," He replied, "yeah she's a looker!" "You banging that?" Angelo asked next. Less than five seconds later he quickly recanted his question and apologized for upsetting LC. Angelo saw the immediate flash of anger in his eyes. Angelo VanDini could not remember the last time he apologized to anyone. That's why he had the two goons with him at all times. Tony and Tony were glad also, they both were uncomfortable with what they saw in LC's eyes also.

LC was more amazed than those three were. He could not believe that he let his emotions get the best of him and that they played out as easily as they did. He liked being in total control of his feelings and how he expressed them. He also realized that Kassaundra had more of a grip on his heart than he thought.

He apologized back to them and stated that he apparently had more feelings for her than he was aware of. Both Tony's looked like bookends. The larger of the two by five pounds stated that he could understand why he would feel that way because Kassaundra was very attractive and added, "Kassaundra is a very nice person, and she has always been very nice." Now LC knew why Angelo did not let them talk much. Big Tony put his foot in his mouth and didn't even know it. LC let it fly right over his head.

LC ordered cocktails for the four of them from the average looking flight attendant. He then shook their hands and told him he appreciated their concerns. Then he stated, "Unfortunately, it'll never work out." Angelo asked, "Why not?" LC replied, "Because she's a cop." He explained to them that his entire life he had tried to do everything by the book and all he had was his pension to show for it. "Now I move out to Vegas looking for some different action and who do I get hooked on, a gorgeous cop."

Angelo asked LC what he meant by different action. LC replied, "I don't really know, maybe something that is completely legal, but anything that pays well enough that I won't have to make these express flights back to Philly just to hold on to what I got." LC thought to himself that the statement he just made sounded open enough; he also liked the direction it was going. He then added, "I don't want to hurt anyone physically if I can help it, maybe some white collar bullshit."

He then told them that he was sorry for boring them with his inability of not being more successful in life than he wanted to be. LC added, "Probably the booze talking and the realization that I'd better enjoy this first class seat, cause thanks to your generosity Angelo, my trip back to Vegas will be the last luxury flight for me."

Angelo looked at LC for 15 or 20 seconds and then made the remark LC was hoping for. "Perhaps I can show you a way to make some easy money." LC replied, "I would be happy to listen to any suggestions." Angelo started to explain, "What I tell you is between us. The fat Tony twins here and myself are the only ones who know who all is involved. Most of the people that are in on this are not aware of the scope of it." He continued, "Some might suspect others but we don't talk about that. The least you know of the involvement of others the safest it is for them and you and no one needs to get hurt." LC thought to himself that this was mostly propaganda. He was sure everyone that was downstairs in the billiards room at the Sander's house knew about each other and probably much more. Angelo started again, "At this point all you will have to do is pick up a package at one location designated by me and drop it off at another location with no questions asked, maybe in different cities and maybe not. The better you do, the more successful we become. The more pick ups and deliveries you make the more money you can make." LC cut in, "Angelo, I should have mentioned this before, if this involves drugs, I'm out." Angelo quickly responded, "No, no, I don't deal in drugs of any kind. In fact I encourage my people to stay away from dipping their fingers or noses in any of that illicit behavior because they just get stupid and talk too much, and we don't want any of that. I will let you know more of the contents of the packages at a later date after I check out a few things." LC knew that what he really meant was that he had to check him out further. LC gave Angelo a secure cell phone number at his request so he could contact him when his services were needed. He also informed him that he originally intended to return to Vegas by the weekend. "I might have a package for you to take back with you," Angelo added.

CHAPTER 11
The Partners

L C checked in to a decent but not lavish motel in a better section of Philly. Before unpacking or getting cleaned up he called his lawyer and had him set up an appointment with his partners at his office. When Jullio's secretary answered she squealed with delight when she heard his voice. LC wondered if his life long friend Attorney Jullio Achille was fooling around with her or not, but always the gentleman and professional lawyer he denied any misdoing. The meeting was set for 7:00 that evening.

A quick shower and an original Philly sandwich and LC felt on top of his game. He had rented a car at the airport and was on the way to Jullio's office. He stopped and bought three Macanudo cigars and a couple Partagas for himself for the next day. He had been smoking cigars for 40 years and his lungs were still crystal clear. He didn't inhale them but that still poked a hole in the secondary smoke bullshit theory.

Jullio greeted him at the front door of the office building as it was after hours and the place was mostly deserted. After a handshake and a friendly bear hug LC gave him one of the cigars. Standing inside the lobby behind the tinted windows LC glanced outside just in time to see little Tony drive by slowly. LC pointed him out to Jullio and the Attorney's brain immediately kicked in and he came out with his last name and crimes committed.

Once secure inside Jullio's office he shook hands with the other two individuals invited to the meeting, Judge Shane Connelly and Philly Police Chief Charles Powers. LC had played football with both men and they had been friends forever but he chose not to travel in their inner circle. That's why he was both stunned and flattered when they approached him with a problem they thought existed, and they were right.

LC handed the Judge a cigar, his snipper and his lighter. Three of the men happily puffed away and laughed at Chuck's complaints of the room rapidly filling with smoke. The Chief had always been a physical fitness nut and would never consider taking foul smelling cigar smoke into his lungs. Jullio had a $3000.00 overheard air filtering system but gleefully waited awhile before turning it on. The room cleared immediately but Chuckie was still coughing much to the delight of the other three.

Attorney Achille, Judge Connelly and Police Chief Powers had many discussions among themselves over the past three years that was a carbon copy of what Captain Cimini from Vegas had discussed with LC. Law enforcement personnel making $50,000 a year and living in big houses and driving fat cars was impossible unless they received an inheritance or hit the lottery. The "how" and "why" of it was the puzzle they could not solve. Jullio brought up LC's name to them when he mentioned his impending retirement. They approached him with the same kind of offer that Captain Cimini initiated to LC in Vegas. LC wasn't sure if he wanted to get involved with it or not but when he found out the names of two of the eleven Philly cops that were suspected his mind was made up. They were the same two assholes that tried unsuccessfully to sully his good name. They were living way above their means and they were very arrogant. LC had the patience of a saint. He would find out the "how and "why" if it took an eternity.

Chief Powers had outfitted LC with all the latest equipment. He had listening devices, cameras and a cell phone that recorded every conversation. This high tech equipment was all donated to him by the manufacturers and had been sitting in his office collecting dust. No one else knew of their discussions or of the intended use of the equipment. Electronic devices always stumped LC. After a lot of trial and error he found that if he pointed the listening cone affixed with a laser pointer he could listen in and record a conversation three blocks away.

The two lowlifes were Jack Whitford and Jim Stimpo. After tailing them for a week he found out that they had contacts in Las Vegas. He also was aware that those contacts were Vegas cops. LC suggested a trip to Vegas was essential to reveal more of the scheme. His friends concurred and he was off.

Three days later LC was flying to his favorite vacation destination. He saw no reason not to mix business with pleasure. He found out that the off duty policemen hung out at the Looney Tune Café.

LC brought his compadres up to date. He told them about Mike Zipp and Jackson Thomas. He mentioned Kassaundra Johnson but only in passing. He talked of the offer Captain Cimini made to him. He spoke of the party and the sneaking around in the Sander's house. When he mentioned Angelo VanDini, the two Tony's, the flight back to Philly and Angelo's offer of easy cash his partners were dumbfounded.

Either through coincidence or pure dumb luck LC had stumbled on the mother lode. His Attorney friend Jullio had a mind like a steel trap. Once inside it stayed there and Jullio had instant recall to it. He informed the group of Angelo's crimes of diamond fraud. Of how he would charge exorbitant prices for excellent one carat or more diamonds but install cheaper inferior stones in the settings instead. He would write up a fancy Guarantee of Value form and figured no one would be the wiser. He would also sell them the insurance for them. He figured that if he was ever confronted about it he would stand on his excellent reputation and tell authorities that the consumer must have had the stones switched. Angelo never figured on a sting set up to get him. Two undercover cops posing as lovers bought a 2.5 carat diamond engagement ring from him. They played it up that they were so happy with their purchase and so much in love. They walked about fifty feet away where a professional jeweler sitting in an undercover car took one look at it and informed them that it was junk. Jullio finished with, "The greedy bastard got 8 years at Graterford."

LC declared that he thought diamonds were still Angelo's topic of choice for his illicit dealings. He went more into detail and related to his partners about seeing something bright and shiny on the pool table and how it was quickly hustled away before he got to the bottom of the stairs. He also mentioned seeing Beverly Sanders with a jeweler's eye piece in a small room behind the bar when he snuck down the steps before hiding under that pool table. LC then related to them what Captain Cimini said about Beverly going to jeweler's school to learn the trade.

Chief Powers asked, "LC, you trust this Captain Cimini?" "Yes, 100%" LC replied, "And two others, officers Mike Zipp and Jackson Thomas. I never saw any of the cops that were at that party before that night. Apparently they don't hang out at the Looney Tune Café. Cimini wanted me to play down my friendship with Mike and Jackson and I agreed with his reasoning.

"Does he know about us?" The Judge asked. "No," LC responded, "I could trust him with it, but I couldn't see a reason to tell him about you three reprobates."

"Oh! By the way," the chief sat up in his chair, "I heard a rumor, supposedly the Justice Department has an inside agent working on this same case."

CHAPTER 12
The Product

Angelo VanDini called LC on Wednesday around 3:00 in the afternoon and invited him to dinner at an Italian restaurant, Bovini's On the Square. LC called Jullio to inform him of his hot date. He knew Jullio would relay the info to the others. He then called Captain Cimini in Vegas and related to him what had transpired since arriving at McCarran Airport before departing for Philly. He said nothing about his Philadelphia associates. He could trust him but it was still something that needn't be discussed and why confuse the issue.

Entering the restaurant LC immediately saw Angelo and little Tony sitting at a round table in the rear. The entire scene looked like a setting from one of the Godfather movies. Everything he saw or everyone he spoke to ended with a vowel. Approaching the table he noticed that there were two extra place settings. Little Tony pushed out a chair for him to sit in, LC walked around and sat at the other one. They exchanged greetings and LC asked where big Tony was by commenting, "Where's your fat twin, on a diet?" The two men burst out laughing.

Angelo asked LC if he had a chance to see his attorney yet. LC replied that he had seen him the first night in town. "He had me come in 7:00 Monday night and sign a bunch of papers. He's got me investing my IRA in something. I'm sure he's making money off me some how as anxious as he was to see me. He wants me to stop back before I leave to look at some projections or something." LC was amazed how easily the lies flowed from his lips, but then again he knew Angelo was already well informed of his visit to Jullio's office.

The topic of conversation was limited mostly to just small talk. LC did find out that Angelo was a big cigar fan also. The food was very good and LC was perusing the dessert menu when big Tony made his arrival. He faked an apology for being late, sat down and ordered enough food to feed Ethiopia for a month. Angelo blurted out, "So much for the diet, Huh!" Big Tony's puzzled look made them laugh even louder.

LC had a suspicion that big Tony was late because he was probably shaking down LC's motel room. There would have been nothing to find. LC kept all the high tech equipment given to him by the Chief in a rented storage shed and he had that key in his pocket.

LC pulled out cigars for Angelo and himself. Their earlier conversation revealed that neither Tony smoked. Angelo thanked him politely and nodded to little Tony. He stood up and Angelo asked LC to accompany him to the men's room. LC stated, "I'll help him wash his hands but that's all." Angelo chucked and responded with, "I just want to be cautious and 100% positive I'm making the right decision here. He's just going to check you for a wire." LC said he understood and was glad little Tony wasn't kinky or something.

In the men's room LC took his shirt completely off and dropped his pants to his ankles. He asked little Tony if he wanted him to drop his drawers also. "I might have an antenna taped to my penis," LC declared. When they returned Angelo asked little Tony if he saw anything suspicious, "Just a lot of muscle on a guy that's ten years older than me," he responded. LC smiled and simply said, "Twenty."

Angelo VanDini made up his mind and sealed his fate at the same time. "Okay, here's the skinny. The majority of time you'll be transporting jewelry, expensive diamonds or worthless paste. Keeping you in the dark of the actual value you will be carrying should deter you of any thoughts of taking off with the merchandise." LC responded, "Hey! I know what to do with money but I don't have a clue what to do with diamonds and such."

Angelo asked LC when he planned on heading back to Vegas. LC told him, "Anytime after my next meeting with my lawyer which I hope is tomorrow. I hate to admit it but I am kinda missing that Kassaundra girl." LC was finding it easier and easier to lie but that last statement was all truth. Angelo said, "Why don't you book your flight back around 10:00 Friday morning and I'll have a package for you to take back and give to my daughter. There also will be $500 for your services with it." LC answered, "That's what I'm talking about. I love it when a plan comes together."

LC called Jullio to set up an appointment at 5:30 early Thursday evening. He instructed him to make up some phony investment papers for him to sign just in case Angelo needed further convincing. He wanted them also to show Kassaundra. Attorney Achille replied, "I'll do better than that. Since you are getting paid from us, Captain Cimini and now Angelo, we might as well reinvest your portfolio." Whatever the hell that meant. LC cut in, "I knew you'd get me one way or the other."

LC met with Jullio Thursday afternoon and filled him in on what transpired at the restaurant. Then Jullio had him sign his name 14 times. LC asked, "Which one of these puts you in my will?" Jullio replied, "None of them but you did just adopt me. Do you have a will?" LC replies, "I'm amazed you didn't think of that also." Jullio then presents a form from his file cabinet, "Here take this and fill in the blanks and mail it to me. Seriously Lassiter, this is something you need to do, especially now."

LC did have two daughters, one loved him and one hated him, thanks to his ex-wife. They were both very successful and didn't need his pittance.

Six AM Friday morning LC awoke to someone lightly tapping on his door. He cautiously opened the door to a red eyed, yawning big Tony. "Here," He said, "There are instructions inside." And off he went.

LC opened the bag. It resembled a bank's night deposit bag only fancier. Inside was a small square purse containing 37 diamonds; at least they looked like diamonds. There was a bank envelope containing $500 in $20 bills and a very official Diamond Courier License with his picture on it. And lastly a short note to get them to Beverly Sanders' house within an hour after touch down at McCarran Airport in Vegas. He was instructed to give them directly to her and she would be expecting them.

There was one more item in the bag that was probably overlooked by VanDini. It was a small piece of scrap paper. It appeared to be the right hand bottom corner of a form. It had 117 on it. Something jarred LC's mind but he couldn't quite put his finger on it.

The picture on the courier's license intrigued LC. Where did Angelo VanDini get that picture? LC was starring at the photo and a much younger LC was starring back. Just like that it hit him. This was a photo from LC's prison ID.

CHAPTER 13
The Plot

L C made it through airport security without being challenged. He was sure the courier's license was legit, but his prison badge that he still carried was probably the reason for the free pass.

He went into a stall in the men's room. He had already put the $500 with the rest of his money in three different pockets. This had been a habit of his whenever he went on vacation and carried a lot of cash. LC then placed the small purse containing the diamonds in the inside pocket of his sport jacket. Normally he would only be wearing sandals, shorts and a knit shirt to Vegas but he figured he should look the part of a diamond courier so he dressed up some.

He got situated in his first class seat and was sipping on a tall screwdriver with a splash of grenadine in it. He sat the drink down and opened his carry on and took out the fancy bank bag. He kept it partially hidden under the flap of his jacket but no one seemed to notice his actions anyway. LC opened it up and retrieved the small piece of paper with the numbers 117 on it. He was wondering why he immediately thought it was a form number. After looking at it much closer with his bifocals on he could make out what looked like the right hand side of the letter "M" in front of the numbers. That verified his thoughts of it being form 117 but where did that fit into his memory bank?

He then opened up his wallet and looked at his last issued prison ID card with his picture on it. He compared it to the older picture of a younger LC on his courier's license. The newer one he had posed in his Supervisor's uniform and the older one he had been in civvies. LC chuckled to himself reliving in his mind those first few years he got stuck strip searching every asshole that came in on his shift. And also how he had to visually check every asshole's asshole and have them squat and cough. This was done to eliminate any contraband smuggled into the prison via that route. Then he and his partner for that day would give them a uniform, socks, underwear and a pair of sneakers. Then they would document the clothing, jewelry, money and personal items that the new inmate had with him upon his entry into Graterford Prison. They then received a starter kit with a comb, toothpaste, toothbrush and other hygiene products along with a pen, pencil, envelopes and a few stamps. It was just enough to get them started until they could purchase items from the commissary.

The Captain's voice came over the intercom to stay in your seats and fasten your seat belts as they were coming into some turbulence.

LC hated to spill a drink so he quickly downed his and fastened his seat belt. His actions were none too soon as the plane hit an air pocket and dropped about twenty feet. That sudden jarring motion brought form 117 to the front of his brain for immediate recall. Form 117 was used to document any jewelry that was taken from new inmates. The only thing they were allowed to keep was their wedding bands. The inmate was then given the pink copy as his receipt. Upon his discharge any property he had along with any jewelry was returned to him.

A couple years before LC's retirement the Warden came out with a new policy where in all jewelry would be locked up in his new safe. Only he and the Deputy Warden knew the combination to that safe. This was a slap in the face to the guards and supervisors because that basically meant that they were not to be trusted. LC however, was agreeable with what the Warden did. It was one of the few times he agreed to anything he did. LC explained to the other supervisors that if anything ever came up missing that they would be off the hook.

A slow grin came over LC's face as a light bulb clicked on in his brain. He wondered if it was possible that the only two people in the world that he hated in his entire life could be mixed up in something illegal. He could only hope but the joy of bringing them down was worth much more than the money he was being paid for what he found out. The irony of it was amazing. Here VanDini is paying him to deliver a package and unknowingly it incriminates those two assholes. LC would still have to find a way to prove it, but at that moment, life was very good.

Another idea came to him and he decided to play it out. He immediately called Captain Cimini from his car after he deplaned. LC explained to him some of the events but he needed to see him in about an hour if that was possible. They decided to meet at the same place as before. He then headed directly to the Sander's residence.

As LC drove into the driveway he noticed that the garage door was open. The only car inside was a Cadillac with a license plate "Bev-Sand" on it. He decided to walk around the back to the pool area. The security fence was about eight foot high but he could see over the gate when he got closer. Beverly was lying face down on a chase lounge apparently sunning herself, and she was topless. He backed up about fifteen feet and called out her name, she answered, "I'm back here."

LC had politely given her about fifteen seconds to cover up. She called out to him, "LC, I'm back by the pool." He opened the gate and walked through. Beverly was now sitting up and had made no effort to cover herself. He apologized and regretfully turned around. She asked him, "Do you find me disgusting?" "Hell no," He replied, "But you are a married woman." It was a true statement but it still sounded lame. Beverly continued her torture of LC, "Are you blushing?" she asked as she slowly put on her top which didn't cover much. LC asked if Dave was home knowing that he wasn't and she assured him that he was at work. She said, "Let's go downstairs." The temptation was overwhelming, not only from the sexual overtones but also from the standpoint of him finding out exactly how the diamonds fit in, although he had an idea about that. LC said, "Your father told me to give these directly to you; there are 37 of them," and he handed the small purse and contents to her. She casually sat them on a small, round table. He asked her, "Don't you want to count them?" She coyly asked him to come in and they could count them together. Beverly was standing just inches away from LC. He could feel her heat and smell the sun lotion on her fine body. He could also smell the alcohol on her breath. LC was certainly not intimidated by her brazen attitude or her closeness but he pretended that he was. "I'm out of here," he announced and scurried away. He could still hear her laughter when he got to his car. He made a silent vow to settle with her later.

LC met with Captain Cimini at the same diner. He went over everything more thoroughly and added the recent events that just took place at the Sander's residence. "You are a better man than me LC, I'd still be at her house," Cimini stated pumping out his chest. "Yeah, and I would have had to call 911 for you about a half hour ago," LC replied.

LC then showed the fancy deposit bag to the Captain. The bottom 75% of it was a canvas like material. There was a thick plastic or vinyl shell encompassing the top. When he handed it to Cimini he was careful to only handle the bottom part of the bag. "Captain, I don't know if there is someone you can trust enough to obtain finger prints from this top section or not. They might me too smeared to lift a good one and I need it back as soon as possible, Beverly might ask me for it."

Captain Cimini then informed LC that he had a card in his pocket with an agent's name on it from the Justice Department. Apparently they have an interest in this investigation also. I'll contact him and have them analyze the bag. He then asked LC if he had told anyone about their undercover dealings. "Well Gaylord, this is as good a time as any to tell you what's been going on back in Philly." LC told the Captain all about his partners back East and their suspicions and the criminal background of VanDini and his cohorts and how he ended up coming out to Vegas. He also informed him that they had asked him if he trusted this Captain Cimini. "And what did you reply to that?" Cimini asked still astonished by his admissions. "I told them I could trust you completely along with Mike and Jackson." Cimini quietly said thank you. LC then told him that Chief Powers had informed him also that there was an undercover agent working this same case for the Justice Department.

Cimini didn't ask LC if he was getting paid from his Philadelphia connection also. LC thought for a moment about giving him the $500 in twenty dollar bills that he received with the rest of the contents in the bag from big Tony. That had happened in Philly and that would be a different jurisdiction anyway. He knew the Justice Department would make him give it up. He also knew that a professional private investigator would hand that money over as evidence, but LC was doing this as a favor on both ends and he quickly dismissed his thoughts as foolishness.

The Captain then asked LC if he had an idea of exactly what crimes were being committed and how those diamonds and jewelry fit in to the whole scheme.

LC replied that he had repeated the words VanDini had told him from the conversation at the restaurant over and over in his mind. The fact that there are real diamonds, fake diamonds and jewelry involved led him to believe that the expensive stones were being replaced by the junk stones in the jewelry pieces. Where the jewelry originates from is the question and his next step in his investigation. He was pretty sure he had brought back fake stones from Philly. He certainly was no expert but he didn't think they would trust him with 37 high quality diamonds on his first run. Also, Beverly wasn't concerned in the least about counting them.

He then asked Cimini what Dave Sanders job description was at the precinct. Cimini replied, "He's in charge of the Property and Evidence Division. He started out as a patrolman and a damn good one but then he supposedly hurt his back on the job. When he felt a little better we put him in the P&E room. He was there about six months and the Sergeant in charge retired. Dave had performed so well in there that we put him in charge of the whole shebang with the retiring Sergeant's blessing." LC then asked, "Where does Kassaundra work?" Cimini replied that she had worked everywhere and had done everything they had asked her and she was an excellent officer. When Dave Sanders and Manny Ruiz and their wives went to Paris last year on vacation we put her in Property and Evidence. She had only two days training in there before Dave left and she performed those duties as good as he had done.

CHAPTER 14
The Pleasure

L C was glad his immediate business was over for the day; at least he hoped it was. As soon as he entered his apartment he dropped his luggage and picked up the phone. He was excited to hear Kassaundra's sweet voice even if it was just her answering machine. He left a message for her to call him upon her return. He checked his watch and figured she must be at work. If she got home around 4:30 as usual he would have time to unpack, shower and catch a two hour nap.

LC awoke 45 minutes after lying down. He fell asleep immediately and woke up refreshed. He didn't know if he had thought it or dreamt it but every fact was now clear in his mind. He figured the jewelry came from two different sources. The Las Vegas Police Department Property and Evidence room and the Graterford Prison Property room in Philadelphia.

If his thinking was correct, Dave Sanders, Kassaundra and a few other officers brought their work home. LC was sure they would drop off the jewelry at the Sander's residence, or if Dave worked he would just take it home with him. Beverly would then analyze the worth of the stones in the jewelry and replace the high quality ones with the junk ones.

Back in Philly Angelo VanDini would receive jewelry from new inmates coming into the correctional system. He then would perform the same service as his daughter, swapping the quality stones for fake ones. With a little luck his couriers would be the Warden and/or the Deputy Warden. Those two being handcuffed, arrested, found guilty and incarcerated would bring him more pleasure than a hundred orgasms.

Besides the locations of the crimes the difference between the two would be the length of time VanDini and his daughter had to make the swap. In the prison system a new inmate and anyone with access to the paper work would know how long their sentence would be. VanDini would have plenty of time to do his illegal alterations. In fact, there would be a huge back log of jewelry in the Warden's safe.

At the Police Station in Vegas the majority of criminals would only be spending a few hours there. They would be bailed out, released or sent to the Clark County Prison. LC wondered if Dave Sanders had an accomplice at Clark County. He also wondered if VanDini had any other children or friends doing the same thing in other cities. He might have a whole friggin' franchise system going on like McDonalds or something.

LC jumped out of bed and hurriedly threw on a pair of shorts, sandals and a shirt. He decided to follow Kassaundra when she left work to see if she happened to make a side trip to the Sander's house.

His timing couldn't have been better. He located her car parked in a ramp about a block away from headquarters. He shut the engine off, looked again in his rear view mirror to make sure of his viewing angle and reached for a cigar. He clipped the end of it off, lit it and took a couple puffs. He never inhaled the stogies he smoked but he definitely enjoyed them. His monthly supply of Mr. B's had been waiting for him when he returned from Philly. LC thought they were the best cigar in comparison to price sold by the J.R. Cigar Company out of North Carolina. He took another puff, looked in his mirror and saw Kassaundra's shapely gam slipping in behind the wheel of her car.

Tailing someone was a new experience for LC. He hit one red light and he was now about two blocks back. One thing he knew for certain, she wasn't heading straight home. She also drove past the road that would have taken her in the direction of the Sanders. Looking over the cars in front of him he could not see her Chevy Lumina, he could however, make out a directional sign for the Clark County Prison.

LC picked up his cell phone and called Captain Cimini on his cell phone. He observed Kassaundra strutting into the Clark County Courthouse, which was connected to the Prison. Cimini answered and LC immediately asked him if he knew if Kassaundra had any acquaintances at the court house or the prison. Before the Captain could reply LC cut him off and said, "I'll call you back!"

LC observed Kassaundra walking with two large men in correctional uniforms. He was about 300 feet away but he thought they looked familiar. Maybe he saw them at the party at the Sander's house that night. Suddenly his view was blocked by a Unit 13 Las Vegas Police Department patrol car. He quickly went from being pissed to laughter when he observed Officer Michael Zipp flipping him the bird.

LC grabbed his keys, locked his doors and slipped into the back seat of the cop car. He slumped down in the seat so he wouldn't be seen by Kassaundra and her friends. She was totally engrossed in their conversation and didn't notice Unit 13 drive by. LC asked Jackson, who was driving, if he knew either of the two men she was talking to. They both replied that they didn't know their names but recognized them from working at the prison when they would drop off reprobates there at the intake desk.

Jackson, Mike and LC shot the bull for the better part of an hour. LC filled them in on a few details that Cimini had forgotten but he had kept them well informed. Mike admitted that if he had gotten a chance to get next to Kassaundra he would be a diamond passing fool. The men chuckled and LC told them that he was wondering when Kassaundra would approach him about being a courier for Beverly and her father. The fact that he was from Philly would make him an obvious choice. He then told them that maybe Kassaundra wasn't aware of the merchandise he had brought back from his little trip. "I might find out within the hour though, I have to get back to my car and get my ass over to her house," He said. He then added, "I'm surprised she hasn't called me yet."

Kassaundra's car was at her apartment when he arrived and knocked on her door. She opened the door and immediately gave him a passionate embrace and lingering kiss. LC was on the receiving end of a very special welcome home gift. He was happy to be back in her arms but something was not quite right. LC thought she had been crying prior to his arrival. Maybe she really missed him but maybe there was another reason. Also, she seemed slightly distracted, as if she had something weighing heavily on her mind. Rather than be his normal loutish self and come right out and ask her he decided to let it simmer and surface on its own.

CHAPTER 15
The Pool Guy

LC asked Kassaundra if she had eaten yet and she replied that she hadn't but wasn't really hungry yet. He told her that he had missed her and wanted to return the pleasure she had given him. He suggested that they should go out somewhere special, some place fancy and celebrate his return and their relationship. She said she had Saturday off so they could go out and relax, have a good time and enjoy each other later on. LC said he would pick her up in a couple hours and told her to make reservations at the restaurant of her choice. He kissed her, patted her on the butt and went out the door.

A block away LC called Captain Cimini and asked if they could meet the next day. He seemed excited about something and immediately blurted out that he had a complimentary tee time at a plush golf course near Lake Las Vega; anything for free excited Cimini. It was near the Monte Lago resort and the tee times were for 9:15 the next morning. He said he ordered Mike and Jackson to his office as soon as they got back from patrol today. "They normally get back around 5:00 but they never returned until 6:30 because they were bullshitting with you. We need a fourth, can you make it?" He asked. LC replied, "Hell yea, count me in."

The night out with Kassaundra was better than he had hoped it would be. LC was on his third Southern Comfort

Manhattan when the entrée arrived. Kassaundra had informed him that this restaurant in the Boulder's Station Casino served the best prime rib in Vegas. One thing was certain; it was definitely a huge piece of quality meat. He had ordered the king cut, 32 ounces and 4 inches thick, and he knew at least half of it would be his dinner tomorrow night after his golf match.

LC really needed this pampering. He was totally relaxed and enjoying the evening with his very lovely companion even though she was up to her armpits in crime soup. After a great meal they went into the lounge for his favorite after dinner drink, a Stinger. They danced to a couple slow songs and before they got carried away with each other they decided to go and gamble for awhile. An hour later LC had won $180.00 playing Blackjack. That more than paid for his evening so far. Kassaundra liked the poker machines and she said she was up about $50.00.

The happy couple then drove over to the Looney Tune Café for a nightcap or two. Mike and Jackson were there and the three men talked openly about their golf match the next morning. They failed to mention who their fourth player was. Tommy Thompson started bitching out LC for not coming around as much as he used to, "Business has been falling off lately," he said. "Well, for free drinks and top billing I might be persuaded to come in more," LC replied.

LC thought about what Captain Cimini suggested about distancing his friendship in public with the two young patrolmen. Since Kassaundra was the only link between the two camps and she was the one that introduced them he figured the hell with it.

Upon their return to Kassaundra's apartment the two lovers became enrapt like a can of worms. The passion was more intense than the night of the party. Of course, that night his horniness started out by the pool watching the scantily clad show girls running around.

LC knew that his next action would involve getting a look see into the small room behind the bar at Dave and Beverly's house. He would talk to Cimini about that tomorrow. He had other business to take care of now.

The next morning the four men were sitting in their golf carts in the shade waiting for the fairway to clear to tee off. LC had already informed them as to what had transpired to date. He felt it was important that they all keep on the same page. He then told them that he had to find out what exactly was in the small room behind the bar at the Sander's residence. If not him, then maybe someone else he could trust. He thought of having a small camera, maybe a video recorder would be even better to record anything that might be able to be used as evidence at a later trial date.

As the four men discussed their dilemma, Jackson glanced over through the trees at one of the many million dollar homes that were built along the course. He was mindlessly watching a swimming pool serviceman working in the back of the house. "Hey," Jackson jumped up, "What about disguising yourself as a pool guy?" LC replied that it was a great idea but if either owner were home at the time they would know that it was him. He doubted if he would be able to pull off the charade.

Captain Cimini came up with the answer. He stated that his nephew and his girlfriend had been in town for about six months now. "He wants to be a cop, can you believe that?" Cimini then told them that he has been working for a swimming pool service company to earn money until he can take his police test. "He's a great kid, fairly level headed and I think he could keep his cool in a tight situation." Mike quipped that he must come from his wife's side of the family. Cimini continued undaunted, "His name is Izzy and his girlfriend's name is Andrea."

LC had a nice drive down the middle and turned around laughing, "Don't tell me his name is Izzy Cimini?" The captain explained that his real name was Israel, "He was named after Daniel Boone's youngest son. He is from my wife's side, his last name is Cyparski. That was her maiden name." Once again, as the other three men laughed heartily, Cimini failed to see the humor.

The men found out that Izzy and Andrea came out here from Cleveland, Ohio. She got a job as a cowgirl, dancing in a show at the Westward Ho Casino and Motel. "I only saw her twice," Cimni said, "but she's a looker."

The captain said he would try and set up a meeting with his nephew that night around 7:00 or 7:30. He also suggested, but it sounded more like an order, that everyone should be there. Mike chirped up, "If his girlfriend is nice looking, me and Jackson will definitely be there. I'll be there with bells on my toes and Jackson will come with a bone in his nose." "I'll give you a friggin' bone," and the other men laughed as Jackson chased Mike around the cart about five times.

Captain Cimini called LC around 5PM and gave him the address and directions to Izzy's apartment. LC pulled up out front at 7:10 still burping the 18 ounces of prime rib he wolfed down from last night's doggie bag. A smiling Izzy opened the door and vigorously shook LC's hand. "I've heard about ten stories of your escapades already from the guys, my stomach is killing me," Izzy informed him. "They are all lies," LC replied.

As soon as the ruckus died down the Captain explained in detail what the plan consisted of. "The main problem I see at this time is how are we going to get the Sanders to try your pool service?" The men were pondering over this when Izzy asked, "Is that Dave and Beverly Sanders out on Wildwood Drive?" The other four men answered as one, "Yes!" Izzy continued with a shit eating grin, "I already clean their pool every other Monday." Izzy opened up a small appointment book, turned a couple pages, looked up and said, "This Monday at 1:00." LC asked the Captain, "Can I adopt this boy?"

Jackson Thomas had taken electrical engineering as a major at UNLV. Since Beverly Sanders had never met him and Dave would be at work, Jackson would go as Izzy's helper. With equipment supplied by the Captain, Jackson would check for any surveillance cameras or theft protection services and clear them so Izzy could get into the room and record all that he could.

LC asked Jackson, "Do you really know how to do all that?" Jackson replied that with the proper equipment it was actually simple. Mike immediately piped in, "He's really not as dumb as he looks." The men laughed as Jackson choked him and Mike stuck out his tongue and made exaggerating gagging sounds. The mutual friendship between the two men was again apparent.

Mike's eyes lit up and Jackson immediately released him. Jackson knew him like a book and loved him like a brother. Mike asked, "Hey, why don't we put a tap on their phone and a couple bugs inside?" The Captain agreed that it was a great idea. "He gets smarter when I choke him," Jackson said.

The Captain stated, "It's a great idea, but I'm not sure I can get a judge to sign for a phone tap before noon on Monday, but we'll definitely go with the listening devices." Then he added, "I know of only one judge I can trust completely but he's in Reno till next week."

It was agreed that the men would all meet at 3PM at the Captain's office the next day, everyone except LC. Sunday's were a little slower in the office but LC did not need to be seen there.

When he got home LC called Jullio's cell phone in Philly. The groggy lawyer answered and bitched at LC for waking him. "You old bastard," LC teased, "It's only midnight back there. It wasn't that long ago we would start to party at that time." He then informed him of their plans for Monday. Jullio said that if it were him, he would put a tap on the phone anyway. "You can't use what you learn in a court of law but you will find out important info that might be very useful to get them to trial," He stated. Then he added, "Just don't get caught." LC harassed him about being an underhanded bastard but he loved him anyway.

LC then called Jackson; he was at the Looney Tune Café of course. LC told him what Jullio had said and added that he knew the Captain wouldn't go for it. Jackson replied, "Let me see what I can do. I have some rats that owe me favors. This will be between you, Mike and me and no one else." "Agreed," LC simply answered.

LC needed a shower and a good night's sleep but he decided to call Kassaundra first. A half hour later after the refreshing shower he was on the way to her apartment. He wondered to himself if he would ever grow out of this womanizing, maybe when he got older he thought. He then answered himself out loud, "God, I hope not!" He turned into her driveway with a devious grin on his face.

Captain Cimini called LC the next day after the meeting. He informed him that everything was a go for Monday except the phone tap. He also said that Jackson would keep him well informed as things unfolded during or after the search and for him to stay close to his phone in case they needed something.

Five minutes after one on Monday LC's cell phone rang, they had a slight problem. Beverly was sunning herself on a chaise near the pool but even closer to the door. "Is she wearing her red bikini?" LC asked. Jackson replied "Yea," then quickly asked, "How do you know that?" LC said, "I'll fill you in on that later." Jackson then told him that the doors were wide open and access would be easy if she wasn't lying right there. LC said he would be right over. "As soon as I disappear with her, get in there, take care of business, and get out. I'll keep Mrs. Sanders busy," He added.

LC arrived about 10 minutes later. Izzy and Jackson were carrying suction hoses around back, they both ignored him. He was approaching the pool area when he heard Izzy inform Mrs. Sanders that some guy just pulled in her driveway. LC thought to himself that the statement was a nice touch. Beverly jumped up and ran to the gate when she heard LC call her name. Much to the delight of the workers she stood on her tip toes to hug and kiss his cheek. Beverly Sanders was a very fetching woman and her small red bikini displayed much of her charm.

LC asked her to take a short walk with him, "I have something to discuss with you, but not here in front of the hired help," he disdainfully added as he chuckled inside. Beverly grabbed her wrap and followed LC around front. "Let's talk in my car for a minute," LC said. "Do I scare you that much?" Beverly asked. LC truthfully told her that he thought she was extremely pretty and sexy. "I think talking out here will be easier on my libido," LC added. "This is a quiet street, we could sit in the back," she teased. "Yea and your husband's a cop and carries a gun, get in the front," LC ordered. He opened the door for her; she pouted her lips and slid her cute little butt in the car.

He made up a story about losing too much at the Blackjack table. He told her that he won about 85% of the time but his luck has been terrible lately except for the night he was out with Kassaundra. He quickly added that last part in case she and Kassaundra had talked about their date that night. He once again was amazed how easily he could make up lies. Maybe he wasn't as virtuous as he thought he was but then again he was doing what he had to do to get the job done. He drug out his tale as long as he could, even bringing up certain hands he should have won on and how the dealer got a lucky draw and beat him.

LC then told Beverly that he had hoped she or her father had a courier's job for him. "I have some money in the bank but it's wrapped up in IRA's, I would rather not touch them if I don't have to. I know how I'll get, if I start pulling it out to cover gambling losses I'll get jammed up. Once football season gets here I'll be fine. I used to have a football handicapping website and I played until I was 31 years old, I know that game," LC stated with confidence.

Beverly stated that she and her father probably had something for him to do but she would rather keep him in Vegas. LC leaned over and thanked her with a small peck on the lips. She started to respond with added affection but stopped quickly when she saw Izzy and Jackson carrying out their equipment. LC looked up as Jackson walked past his car. He noticed for the first time that Jackson had added a thin mustache to change his appearance. LC almost laughed out loud; Jackson looked like a fat David Niven.

CHAPTER 16
The Pimp

LC backed out of the driveway and waved goodbye to Beverly Sanders. He thought of driving over to Kassaundra's house to get relief from the pressure in his pants caused by Beverly's closeness in the car. He then remembered that Kassaundra was working nights this week on a stakeout.

He stopped at the Looney Tune and had three quick beers and a sandwich. Tom was glad to see him and had bought two of the three beers. He then went home for some R & R.

About 9:30 that night he decided to call her and see what time she was getting off. She answered her cell phone and as always was excited to hear his voice. She informed him that she was working a 12 hour stakeout from 6PM to 6AM. LC was pissed, if he would have known that he could have been at her house at 3:00 in the afternoon. He kept his cool though because he knew she needed her sleep. Kassaundra eased his frustrations by inviting him down to sit in the car with her. She said, "If you are in the car with me between the two of us we will have at least two eyes watching for thieves." LC knew what she meant. He was still talking to her heading out the door; the pressure in his lap was back.

The directions Kassaundra gave him were perfect, he found her with no problem. He parked his car a block away and walked back to hers. The area they were in was a very plush business section of Vegas. They were surrounded by tall glass buildings made up of professional high rises.

After about 15 minutes of small talk the two lovers let nature take its course. About 10 minutes into their amorous groping, with their clothes still intact, a dark van pulled cautiously into the far end of the lot. LC saw it first as Kassaundra was oblivious to anything except LC's affection. They both slouched down in their seats. The van hesitated for a moment before slowly driving away.

Kassaundra decided to pursue it at a very easy pace. She was more interested in obtaining the license plate number. LC suggested that he should get out and stay on the stakeout just in case the van was a decoy. Kassaundra agreed and after LC exited her undercover cruiser he watched as she drove well out into the street before turning on her head lights.

LC could still see her car when he felt an ominous presence near by. A quick scan revealed his plight. He was immediately reminded of that old saying, "Did you ever get the feeling the whole world was a tuxedo and you were a pair of white socks?"

LC was surrounded by four very large men. Just when he was deciding which one to hit first a large red limo appeared from nowhere. All five men stopped in their tracks with their mouths agape. It was if they were looking at a UFO. The limo stopped suddenly and after a moments hesitation the moon roof opened and up popped the ET.

He had a voice LC vaguely recognized. "LC, the last time I saw you, you were in the same predicament," the tall well dressed figure stated.

LC couldn't make out exactly who it was as he was partially blinded by the head lights. The driver and passenger doors opened in unison, and two men dressed alike got out.

The savior standing in the moon roof summoned LC to come and get in the back with him. LC started to protest, he didn't like the idea of someone else fighting his fights. "Get in here Lassiter," he said, "These boys need the exercise." LC started to protest again but the giggle of female voices quickly changed his mind.

The rear door opened and LC slid in the back. He took in the entire scene and forgot about everything else in his life. The luxury and elegance of the vehicle, the beauty and class of the two female passengers and a smiling Greg Denny had totally maxed out LC's brain.

Greg was right, the last time LC remembered being with him was at their senior prom. LC was with his girlfriend, who he later married, standing out in front of the dance. They had broken up for a month and when the wolves found out LC was no longer in the picture a bunch of them had asked her out. Barbara was a beautiful lady and had a body to die for. She had dated a few of her suitors but her heart belonged to LC. He didn't have to worry about her; she could more than handle herself in any situation. He pitied the poor fool who would try and grope her without her consent. In those days it was called, "Copping a feel." LC still had scars from their very passionate and very volatile marriage. Two things he knew for certain, she died too young at 21 and the fact that he would still be married to her if she had lived.

Barbara had bit the bullet and called LC and asked him to be her escort. He quickly said yes and apologized for starting the argument. He could not remember why they had argued but he figured it must have been his fault. He knew he loved her dearly and any concession on his part would be greatly rewarded. LC was no dummy.

Anyway, he showed up with her and the three "also ran's" came by themselves. When the dance ended they waited out front for LC. When the action started Greg Denny appeared out of nowhere, just like he did tonight. Within ten seconds the ex-suitors were down and moaning. One of them was knocked out cold. That was the one Barbara hit.

When the two men returned to the limo LC noticed that neither one had a mark on them. They weren't even breathing hard. Both men seemed in good humor as Greg introduced them. Joey I. was behind the wheel and Marty D. sat in the passenger seat. LC was very impressed on how jovial they were and the obvious confidence they displayed. They could have been his offspring and LC would have been proud to claim them.

LC turned his attention back to his old friend Greg Denny. He first met Greg back in grade school in DuBois, Pa. He was amazed Greg knew who he was; it had been 40 years since that prom night. LC asked Greg what he had been up to and stated, "Whatever you have been doing I'd say it has been successful." Then he asked, "What's it cost to rent one of these?" Referring to the luxury chariot he was in. Greg replied, "I don't have a clue what it would cost to rent one, so I just bought it outright."

Then Greg apologized for his bad manners. "This is LiAnne and Ashley," he motioned with his finger, "They work for me, but they are also very good friends." LC then asked the ladies if that were true and teasingly added that they could do better. Their loyalty showed through as they both slid over and showered Greg with hugs and kisses.

LC then ask Greg again what line of work he was in to have such good friends up front and such beautiful friends here in the back. Greg stammered for a second and replied, "Let's just say, I provide a service."

LC was normally a little sharper than he was tonight. A slow wave came over his thinking process and reality set in. His old school chum was a pimp. He apparently was very good at it as LC again checked out his surroundings.

Greg handed LC a glass of champagne. Normally LC wouldn't touch the stuff but it just seemed right tonight. He noticed Greg's watched and commented on it. Greg slid it off his wrist and handed it to LC. He said, "I'd give it to you but it was a gift from the girls here." LC looked it over. It was a Rolex. He flipped it over and saw an inscription on the back. He didn't have his glasses and didn't question the girls when they excitedly told him what it said, "Happy Birthday, love Ashley and LiAnne."

LC handed the watch back to Greg. As he took his last swallow of champagne he glanced out the window and stated, "Ah, I see Kassaundra is coming back." Greg turned a little pale and asked, "Kassaundra Johnson?" LC confirmed that and asked Greg if he knew her. Greg replied that he had been in business for thirty years and had only been arrested once. "That was about six months ago, I spent 28 days in the Clark County Jail thanks to that girl." Then Greg quickly added, "LC I got to go, here's my card, keep in touch." LC jumped out as Greg and his friends drove away.

Kassaundra pulled up just as the thugs started to come around. "Was that who I think it was?" She asked as she placed her handcuffs on the first guy. LC replied, "Greg is and old friend of mine." "Do you do business with him?" Kassaundra asked with sarcasm. "Honey, I haven't seen him in forty years until tonight, he showed up just as these four goons were about to jump me. I couldn't believe he recognized me as quickly as he did. The last time I saw him I had hair," LC replied.

"He exploits women," Kassaundra went on, "and he tried to solicit me to work for him. He's got balls, I'll give him that. I was in my uniform when he asked me if I would be interested in making a career change. Did he help you with these assholes?"

"Not personally, he had me get in the car while his two henchmen took care of these chumps," LC stated. Kassaundra informed LC that Marty and Joey were both heavy weight Golden Gloves champions. She said Marty was one of the top arm wrestlers in the world. Joey was a professional door man at many of the top nightclubs in the US. Then she added, "And they are the nicest, sweetest guys and always perfect gentlemen."

LC agreed with her and stated that the women certainly didn't look used and abused in anyway. He added that the two men in front didn't seem the type to sit back and do nothing if Greg put his hands on them. "Those two have too much integrity for that." Kassaundra didn't say anything but she mentally agreed with the statement LC had just made.

Kassaundra called for backup as LC put plastic ties on the last two assailants. LC stated, "I better get going before your backup gets here, I don't want to get you jammed up." Kassaundra replied, "No relax, Jackson Thomas and Mike Zipp are swinging by to pick these guys up. I'll take two in my car and finish the paper work. I can probably get off early and I'll meet the three of you at the Looney Tune later.

Moments later Mike and Jackson drove up and the baggage was split up and placed in the cruisers. It was decided that Kassaundra would only take one with her per company policy and the other two would go in the back of the men's car. Mike said under his breath, "We'll hear about this later." After promising to meet LC in about 45 minutes they drove off.

"Baby if I can't get off early or get swamped with more paper work, I'll call you," Kassaundra said as she gave LC a peck on the cheek.

The situation was perfect. LC would have a chance to talk to the guys and find out what all was uncovered in the little room at the Sander's house.

CHAPTER 17
The Pay Off

Jackson, Mike and LC sat down at a side table. The Looney Tune wasn't too busy yet and they could talk undisturbed. LC wanted to know what they found in the room. Jackson wanted to know what the story was between LC and Beverly Sanders. Mike wanted to know where Jackson got his little sissy mustache.

LC told them what had entered his mind when he saw Jackson's mustache. "You looked like a fat David Niven." Both men laughed and then asked, "Who is David Niven?"

LC then assured them that Beverly liked to flirt and tease him but that was all that ever happened between them. Both men smiled and nodded but neither believed him. They had seen LC in action too many times.

The conversation then turned serious. Jackson told LC that the only security the Sanders had was the one for the house, but it wasn't turned on. That made sense because Beverly was at home. The video they took was crystal clear and showed bags of diamonds, either real or fake. "There were some pieces of jewelry and about fifty Rolex watches still in their boxes," Jackson added. "Probably generics," Mike said, "I doubt they would have a quarter of a million dollars in watches just lying around."

The men sipped their beers and remained silent for a short time while contemplating their discussion. LC then informed the guys of what had taken place earlier. They were amazed LC knew Greg Denny. They both admitted that they liked Greg and his two bodyguards.

"He treats his people very well, never causes a scene and contributes a great deal every year to the policemen's retirement fund," Mike stated. "We never bother him but Kassaundra arrested him a short while back," Jackson smiled and then added, "I guess he offered her a position she didn't care for." The men laughed again and then ordered three more beers.

"You know LC, Mike and me figured you and Kassaundra got a little rough with those punks tonight, but now you tell us that was Greg's boys that helped you out?" Jackson asked but he already knew the answer. LC replied anyway, "Those guys weren't punks, they were large experienced men. It was four against two and Greg's boys handed them their panties in about fifteen seconds."

The three men closed the bar. Kassaundra might have called but LC saw that his cell phone was dead. He went home for some much needed sleep.

Kassaundra called LC around noon and invited him over around 3:00 that afternoon. LC and his cell phone were both recharged and he immediately accepted her offer.

He hung up and his phone rang again instantly. Captain Cimini was on the other end. He asked LC to come over to his house for a quick lunch and he would show him the tapes that his nephew had taken. LC was familiar with the area and said he could be there in fifteen minutes.

He arrived a short time later and was impressed with the Captain's home. It wasn't extravagant but it certainly was not a shack either. The inside was neat and tastefully decorated. LC remarked that his wife must be very chic and well coiffed as a home usually reflects the appearance of the lady of the house.

His theory was quickly laid to rest as the Captain introduced his bride. Large Marge was a very nice lady and a very good cook as LC soon found out. He complimented her cooking and before she exited the dining room to fetch desserts from the kitchen she graciously thanked him. Cimini simply sighed and whispered low, "She was 115 pounds when I married her."

After lunch the men went into the game room where the Captain had the VCR and the tape ready for viewing. The tape started out showing the entrance from the pool area and progressing down the stairs to the billiard room. LC interrupted, "That's the pool table I hid under." The tape showed the bar area and the small room behind it. The Captain commented that the Sanders must be pretty sure of themselves as Izzy opened the unlocked door. Jackson and Izzy did an excellent job as they took close ups of the diamonds, jewelry and the Rolex watches.

As the camcorder zoomed in on the fake Rolexes, their boxes being opened up by Jackson, the captain stated that he never knew they made so many different ones. The tape soon ended and Captain Cimini said the only problem was how to link the evidence to a crime. "It's not illegal to have what we just viewed in your possession. The pay off for all your hard work will come when we can link that evidence to a crime or some sort of criminal activity." The Captain stated what LC already knew. "What I can't understand is what's with all the Rolexes? I agree with your theory about replacing quality diamonds with junk in the rings and other jewelry, but for the life of me I can't figure out how these Rolexes fit into the picture," the Captain added.

LC thanked the Captain for his hospitality and shook his hand. He then kissed Marge on the cheek and again thanked her for a delightful lunch. He gave her a hug. Well, he gave her half a hug because that is as far as his arms could reach around her.

LC then went back to his apartment to take a shower and call Jullio in Philly. He informed him of what all was on the tape. Jullio didn't have an answer for LC either, as the question of the Rolexes arose. "I'll put on my thinking cap and if you figure it out call me back," Jullio told him.

LC drove over to Kassaundra's apartment, he was glad to give his mind a much needed rest. As soon as he entered she was all over him. Her total display of affection always amazed him. Later after the climax of their passion or the passion of their climax subsided LC watched her wiggle her way out of the bedroom. She soon returned with a sexy kimono wrapped around her lovely lithe body. She handed him a can of beer she was carrying. She then reached into her cleavage and pulled out a Cohiba cigar, clipped off the end of it, lit it and stuck it in LC's mouth. He was not a religious man but he figured this must be what heaven is all about. She turned on the TV for him and instructed LC to relax while she re-showered and started to get ready for work.

LC took a puff and blew a few smoke rings. He glanced at his watch and a light switch clicked on in his head. He wondered to himself just how many high rollers wearing Rolex watches came through Vegas every year. He didn't know if it was the sex, the rest or the cigar but suddenly everything seemed so clear to him.

LC figured that the cops at the Sander's party probably had contacts inside the casinos. Dealers, pit bosses, bartenders and waitresses would alert them to high rollers wearing expensive jewelry. The underhanded men in blue would probably have prostitutes solicit the males and then for one reason or another show up and arrest them.

Or if the whales drove themselves rather than take advantage of a limo comp they would be pulled over for no reason and be arrested for DUI or some other trumped up charge. Then after their arraignment the rich suckers would be taken to the Clark County jail. If the jewelry or Rolexes could be exchanged for the fake ones before the bail bondsman showed up then the switch would be made. The better scenario would be where the unlucky, unenlightened sucker would get a sentence of a few days to a few months then there would be plenty of time to make a switch.

And lastly, all property seized during drug busts, recovered stolen property, etc. would be held in the property room at police headquarters. That of course would be a personal delivery into the hands of Dave Sanders.

As LC slowly got dressed, like always he did a physical inspection of his pocketed items. It had nothing to do with Kassaundra's presence; he just did it out of habit. There in the middle of his money was Greg Denny's card. At this point even more thoughts entered his mind. He said to himself, "Wow! You are on a roll today." He would contact Greg as soon as possible and ask to borrow his Rolex. Greg could come with him if he chose to and have an expert decide the true value of his watch. He hollered in to Kassaundra and said he had to run and that he would call her later.

CHAPTER 18
The Phony

Marty D. answered with, "Greg Denny Enterprises, may I help you?" LC chuckled and replied, "Well Marty, you and Joey I. helped me out the other night so I still owe you guys one."

Marty told him that Joey I. is getting fat and the exercise did him some good. Then he added, "Greg told us stories about you when you two use to run together back in school. We damn near pissed ourselves from laughing so hard."

"Greg always did exaggerate a lot," LC replied. "Is the old asshole available or do I have to make an appointment," He asked. LC overheard Marty ask Joey if he saw Greg yet today and wondered if he was up yet. LC looked at his watch; it was 4:40PM.

Greg came to the phone about two minutes later. LC apologized for waking him if he was still getting his much needed beauty rest. Greg responded that he had been up for an hour already and that he and the girls just finished bathing. "When Marty hollered in to us that you were on the phone the girls told him to have you come right over and get in the tub with us. I think they like you, especially Lianne," Greg added.

LC asked if they could meet and Greg replied that he would have the limo pick him up and they could all go to breakfast. LC laughed and said that he had a small breakfast about 8 hours ago and had a nice lunch about 4 hours ago.

"Well, it'll be about an hour and a half before the girls are ready. If you want to meet before that we can do it," Greg stated. LC replied that he would rather wait a little while anyway. "I'm really not hungry yet and I have something to discuss with the girls if that's all right with you."

"Of course you can speak with them. I don't own them, they are my friends. I would ask them not to charge you if that is the business you wish to discuss with them," Greg stated. LC replied that his business with them had more to do with the Rolex watch they had bought him for his birthday. LC added, "I hate to ask this of them but if they have a receipt from the jewelry store where they purchased the watch, please have them bring it. If it's hot or if they got it from a John or something I don't care in the least. If they did buy it, then we might be on to something and I will discuss that with you later."

LC was immediately upset with himself for implicating that the girls might have done something illegal to obtain the watch. He knew that his choice of words could have been much better. He started to explain that fact to him but Greg seemed to understand completely. Greg got the directions to LC's apartment and said they would pick him up at 7:00PM.

At exactly 7:00PM Joey I. pulled up out front. LC jumped in the back and said his "hellos" all around. Ashley was sitting next to Greg so LC ended up next to Lianne. She put her hand on his leg and with a seductive smile reached into her cleavage and pulled out a piece of paper. Lianne's sexy voice asked LC if this is what he wanted.

LC didn't miss her obvious hint but her action of pulling the receipt from her cleavage brought back the recent memory of the cigar Kassaundra pulled out of hers. He was sitting beside a very lovely woman with obvious charm that no doubt had a magnitude of experience on how to pleasure a man and his mind was on Kassaundra.

LC looked at the receipt. The girls had paid $5888 for the Rolex watch and inscription plus tax. LC asked if Mel's Fine Jewelry Collections was on the way. Marty D. answered from the front passenger seat that it was directly across the street from the restaurant where they were going to eat at.

When they pulled up in front of the restaurant Greg stated that he and the guys would go in and get their table. LC requested his watch and proceeded across the street with the girls.

As they entered the store the three were greeted by a very distinguished gentleman with a 24 carat smile and a name pin to match. Mel recognized the girls and hugged them and vigorously shook LC's hand. He then asked how he could be of help and asked if they would like a glass of wine or something.

LC graciously refused and stated that they had friends waiting for them across the street at the restaurant. He then produced the receipt and asked Mel if it came from his store. Mel replied, "Yes, and this is my writing. I remember when these lovely ladies came in and bought it."

LC then handed Mel the watch and asked him if this is what they paid $5888 for. Mel looked at the watch turning it over twice. "This looks like a phony to me," he announced. He picked up his jewelers eye piece and took a closer look. As soon as he turned it over to look at the inscription he immediately stated that it was not his work.

Mel became upset and wanted to know what kind of game they were playing. He stated that he dealt only in the finest jewelry and what he sold the girls was a genuine Rolex Players watch. He said he could only get three at a time from the manufacturer.

It was obvious to LC that Mel was telling the truth. He wanted to be sure the jeweler was not involved in any shady doings. LC calmed him down and informed him that a switch had apparently been made by someone else and he was simply trying to eliminate the honest people involved. He then asked Mel if he was 100% certain and if he would be willing to testify at a hearing to verify the phony was not his.

Mel calmed down and his smile returned. He said he wanted to show LC something that would validate his claim. "Here is another Rolex, a less expensive model than the Player that these ladies bought. I want you to look through this eye piece at the inscription on the back of this one," Mel stated with a beaming face.

LC clumsily placed the eye piece up to his left eye, the one without the stigmatism, and tried to make out what it said. "If you compare the two," Mel said, "you will see a lack of quality in the printing." LC took his word for it as he could barely make out anything.

Mel told him to move the watch closer or further away until he could see it clearly. He then told LC to look at the small mark he had placed at about 4 o'clock on the outer edge. He then informed LC that because this watch was waiting to be picked up by a customer that had purchased it yesterday, and this was April, he had placed the mark at 4 o'clock. "If this were September," he added, "I would have placed it at 9 o'clock."

"Now look at this fake watch," Mel said as he handed it to LC, "There is no mark at all."

Mel then went into a 5 minute tirade about his reputation and the schools he attended and how many quacks were out there and how long he has been in business. He finally finished up with what LC was waiting to hear, "You're damn right I'll testify," Mel roared out.

LC and the girls thanked him and instructed Mel to keep their findings confidential. "Someone will contact you when the time comes and thanks again," LC stated and shook his hand.

They walked back across the street to the restaurant where the guys were impatiently waiting. Marty told them that Joey I. had eaten three baskets of Italian bread while they were waiting. "He's a growing boy," Greg said with a chuckle.

LC told Greg and the boys what all was uncovered across the street. Greg was upset but not for himself. He felt bad because the girls worked hard for their money and offered to give them $3000 each when they got home. His offer spoke volumes of the kind of man Greg Denny was. And then what really surprised LC was when the girls stated they would not accept it.

The business his old friend and his new friends partake in might be illegal or immoral but they all had integrity and an honest outlook on life. LC knew he could trust them and over a splendid meal he revealed the real reason he ended up in Sin City.

Greg spoke highly of Captain Cimino and Mike and Jackson. He knew LC dated Kassaundra so he politely stopped short of saying what he thought of her.

LC assured them that he would do all he could to get back the genuine Rolex that the girls had purchased. Joey I. drove LC back to his apartment and before exiting the limo he was bombarded by hand shakes and compliments from the guys and hugs and kisses from the girls. He knew he must have been covered in lipstick.

CHAPTER 19
The Press

As soon as LC entered his apartment he called all interested parties in Vegas and Philly and filled them in on the latest events. They all agreed with LC's reasoning about just how the Rolexes fit in to the picture.

He was standing in the kitchen still talking with Jullio when he observed Kassaundra's car pulling into the rear of his apartment complex. LC walked to the back door and unlocked it. He finished his conversation and placed his cell phone on top of the refrigerator next to the toaster. He caught a glimpse of his reflection in the toaster and immediately saw about six partly opened lip prints on his face.

LC did not panic easily but this was crunch time. He opened the refrigerator door and grabbed a half of an orange that he had left over from breakfast. He hastily smeared it all over his face, grabbed a hand full of paper towels and was amazed how easily the dried lipstick came off. He briefly remembered those commercials boasting of the powers of "Orange Plus". LC wondered if he could make one of those commercials. As the orange and paper towels landed in the bottom of the waste basket Kassaundra entered with a devious smile on her face.

LC knew he loved her but he decided it was time to press her about her involvement in all this mess. She kissed him passionately and he decided to press her with something else first.

He knew it wasn't his best boudoir performance but Kassaundra appeared happy none the less.

He started out, "Kass, do you remember when I went to the airport here to buy a round trip ticket to Philly a couple weeks ago?" Kassaundra nodded slowly with an inquisitive look on her face. LC then proceeded to relate to her the details of what took place from the time Angelo paid for his first class seating on the plane until he arrived back in Vegas a few days later. He of course skipped over the part about the meeting with his good friends who represented the law in Philadelphia.

When LC was finished telling her the procession of events adding also his stopping at the Sanders and giving Beverly the pouch her father had given him to deliver, there was a long silence.

Kassaundra got up and went into the bathroom, came back out and never said a word. LC knew women and he also knew the silence would not last. He could tell she was pissed off about something as she got dressed to leave.

She blurted out, "Why the hell would you get involved in something so stupid?" LC replied, "Hey, I can use the extra money same as you."

Another minute or two of silence was soon followed by another outburst. "Yes, but I needed the money desperately, you just want some extra cash to gamble with," she replied. Kassaundra continued, "I did what I had to and I'm sick to my stomach for doing it, but I stopped. I just started feeling better and now I find out the man I love, the one man in my entire life that is honest and has integrity is doing the same stupid shit."

Well, it was out in the open now. LC knew she liked him a lot but the big "L" word just popped out of her mouth. LC was about to mount a rebuttal but noticed a tear rolling down her cheek and he caved in. He held her close and openly confessed his love for her. He promised her he would not make the same dumb mistake again.

He came very close to telling her the entire undercover James Bond bullshit he was involved with but stopped abruptly when Kassaundra planted a big kiss on his lips. One thing led to another and the next bout of torrid love making began in earnest. She was apparently very happy LC shared the same feelings that she had for him.

The next morning he awoke with Kassaundra under his arm with her head against his chest. She looked so peaceful and blissful and LC decided he could get used to her being this close on a steady basis.

He knew his next step would be to pressure Captain Cimini into not pressing charges against Kassaundra. LC would go even farther and demand that she gets to keep her job. His trump card would be his testimony. They probably had enough evidence to get a conviction anyway but LC was positive his testimony would secure it.

Kassaundra left about an hour later after a blissful adieu. LC grabbed his phone from the top of the refrigerator and again glanced at himself in the toaster. He decided a shower was in order and skipped over the thought of obtaining the orange half out of the waste basket. He enjoyed having Kassaundra's lip prints on his face.

Captain Cimini answered his cell phone on the first ring. He told LC that he was just about to call him. "LC," the Captain started, "I decided that any Vegas cops that are not involved too deeply in this investigation we should just forget about. It would take way too much time and money to try and prosecute them on misdemeanors. Plus, the media would have a field day and so would internal affairs. Everyone stumbles from time to time and who knows, maybe this will make better policemen out of them. I don't want the public to lose faith in the fine police force we have here."

Cimini then asked LC if he agreed and was there something else he wanted to discuss. LC replied that he agreed whole heartedly. He stated that Kassaundra should be kept in the clear. He also added, "I don't think the excellent job you have done in putting together one of the best police forces in the country should come under jeopardy."

The Captain thanked him and added, "Kassaundra Johnson is the best cop I've got. That stakeout she was on lead to the arrest of six known felons and the recovery of about $2,000,000 in stolen property."

LC smiled to himself. He was pleased with the Captain's decision and he didn't have to do any begging or bartering. He then asked the Captain how soon he thought the raid and the arrests at the Sander's house would take place.

Captain Cimini replied that he would like it to coincide with the same actions taking place in Philly. That way no one could call and warn the other of their impending doom. LC told him that as soon as their conversation was over he would call his attorney friend Jullio and find out the scoop as too their progress in Philadelphia.

CHAPTER 20
The Philly Fix

J ullio answered the phone with a resounding "Hell-o-o-o LC." He was obviously overjoyed about something. Jullio went on to tell him that thanks to his hard work and his ideas involving the Rolexes that he, the Judge and the Police Chief came up with a great plan. LC replied, "You know you are my favorite ambulance chaser and I love your devious side, so let's hear it."

"Okay, how about this?" The Philadelphia shark was just bubbling. "We have this small time hood named Sal." LC cut in and asked, "What is he an addict or something?"

"He has the same addiction you have; he's addicted to women." Jullio went on, "I think he knows every cop and every Judge and he definitely knows the DA. He is well liked by everyone. Sal would definitely give you a run for your money as a lothario. He attends the policemen's ball every year and sits at one of their tables. Sal always brings a very attractive date and sometimes comes with a police woman. LC cut in again, "Oh! I like this guy already."

"Here's the plan, we call it the ole Philly Fix." Jullio laughed and then continued, "Sal has agreed to be arrested on a possible receiving stolen property charge. He will be wearing my Rolex with a tiny GPS locater inside. Because he has a record he will be taken directly to Graterford on a probation violation. As soon as the locater alerts us that the watch is on the move we'll start the paperwork to get him released. When we know the watch is at Angelo VanDini's home we'll spring Sal and raid Angelo's house and hopefully recover my watch. Of course it will be used as evidence and I won't get it back for six months or so, but it will be worth it.

LC thought the plan was excellent but asked, "What does poor Sal get out of this besides his balls busted and having to look over his shoulder all the time?"

"Oh yea, I forgot to tell you the good news," Jullio stated, "The Chief has offered up a cash for criminals program. It is based on a percentage of stolen property saved or recovered and a few other related details. The maximum amount a person can receive is $300,000. We'll give Sal 10% or $30,000, I'll get the same and you will receive the balance of $240,000."

LC's jaw dropped and he managed to mumble out a thank you. Then Jullio asked LC if he managed to obtain anymore Philly/Vegas links that he got from his planted bugs or his phone tap. LC completely forgot about the phone tap or listening devices that Jackson was going to install the day they were at the pool. He relayed this info to Jullio.

Jullio then hollered into the phone, "If they were planted you've got to get them out of there before they are found in the raid. That possibly could jeopardize the whole investigation. Maybe I can ask Judge Connelly to speak to his golfing buddy. I don't want to mention his name but he is a federal judge and we would have to get his permission for the tap and back date it to the day of the plant. It is a little unethical and illegal but hell, illegal is nothing but a sick bird." Jullio was still laughing at his little joke when LC told him, "You're the sick bird!"

LC hung up and immediately called Jackson. The Vegas patrolman calmed LC down and quelled any anxieties he might have. He informed LC that they had the okay for the bugs but the phone was a skinny cell phone with a blue tooth, "There was no way I could fit it in." LC didn't want to sound stupid so he didn't bother to ask Jackson what he really wanted to know. And that was, "Just what the hell is a blue tooth?"

LC did ask Jackson if anything overheard could be used as evidence. Then he asked, "Who's been listening in all this time?" Jackson politely informed him that this was the 21st. century and listening devices could be recorded for posterity. They could be recorded, re-activated and de-activated by remote control.

"Wait till you hear this," Jackson started. "Mike has been fooling around with this rich, attractive, 50 year old widow." LC replied, "That doesn't surprise me."

The men both chuckle and Jackson proceeds to tell LC that she lives the next cul-de-sac down from the road the Sander's house is on. He explains that her back yard butts up to the Sander's back yard. "Mike is using her back bedroom to record any conversations coming from that little room behind the bar. She enjoys the added attention Mike has shown her plus she likes the idea of being involved in the police work being done there. Of course, she has no idea that we are checking out one of her neighbors."

Happy and content with the way everything was proceeding LC made one more phone call back to Captain Cimini and gave him Jullio's number. He agreed that it was important for both cities' law enforcement personnel to be on the same page. He also thought it was inane to always be the third party so by giving up Jullio's phone number he could eliminate any screw up on his part. The only thing he asked of the Captain was to be kept informed when everything was about to go down.

CHAPTER 21
The Progression of Events

That night LC took Kassaundra down to Laughlin, Nevada for some authentic Mexican food. Afterwards they gambled and LC won $1000 playing a 20 spot Keno card when none of the numbers he selected came in. The casino also offered him a room and breakfasts for two in the morning.

Kassaundra informed him that they had to leave early in the morning as she had to fly to Carson City at 1:15PM the next day. She was a little vague as to her reason why she was going there but LC thought nothing of it and said nothing more.

After a night of rapture LC drove the hour and a half back to Vegas and dropped off Kassaundra. He swung by the Looney Tune Café for a quick beer and drove over to the same restaurant where he, Greg Denny and friends had eaten. LC had a nice breakfast and walked across the street to talk to Mel the Jeweler.

Mel was happy to see him and bolstered LC's confidence about him testifying in court. While he was there he started browsing over the merchandise. LC stated that he had a very special friend and would like to buy her something nice. Mel then asked him which one of those two beautiful women he was with at his store last week was the special one. LC assured Mel that his two companions that day were simply good friends.

Mel replied, "I've been happily married for 35 years but if I had your good friends I wouldn't be married at all.

LC picked out a nice tennis bracelet but was a little shocked at the $1000 price tag. He also told Mel he didn't think his special friend played tennis. Mel politely stifled his laughter and replied, "Well seeing how you are not sure about that I'll let you have it for $400. LC had it inscribed with, "To Kass, Love LC." He was happy with his purchase but thought Mel was a little giddy about something.

Walking back across the street LC lit up a Mr. B's cigar. He was standing next to his car still puffing on his luxurious treat when his cell phone rang. It was Captain Cimini and he informed LC that both raids would be at 8AM the next morning. He also told him that Dave Sanders would be arrested right after roll call but would not be given a phone call until later. If he was stupid enough to call his father-in-law a Philly detective would answer and seal his fate even more.

The next morning LC was up and showered by 9AM. He had to pick up Kassaundra's bracelet. He thought about having breakfast at the same place as yesterday. He loved their food but decided on something healthier. He made himself some coffee, had some wheat toast and an orange. He was still hungry so he cooked some oatmeal. He could eat it if he doctored the shit out of it with cinnamon, raisins, apricots, blueberries, kitchen sink, etc.

LC drove to Mel's Fine Jewelry Collections and picked up the bracelet. Mel had outdone himself on the inscription and didn't charge him a penny more. He had inscribed on the back, "To Kass, the Princess in my life, Love LC."

Mel informed LC that simplicity on a ring is fine because of the lack of space but when there is plenty of room simplicity denotes cheapness. LC thanked him profusely and left as a very satisfied customer.

CHAPTER 22
Poetic Justice

LC was starting to get antsy wondering just how smoothly everything went that morning. He was definitely curious but refused to call the Captain's cell phone if he was still in the middle of something. He thought about calling Jullio but decided to wait for one or both of them to contact him.

About 6:15 that evening Cimini finally called. He informed LC that they arrested Dave Sanders right after roll call that morning as planned. He figured that any of his shady police friends would be out in the streets and would not be able to alert Beverly. "We arrested him at 7:20," Captain Cimini stated, "By the time the raid took place at 8:00 he was crying, admitted to everything and blamed it all on his wife."

LC had judged Dave Sanders all wrong. He thought that Dave was a man's man but in reality he was a sissy. "They are going to love him in prison," LC spoke his thoughts out loud to the Captain.

The Captain continued, "I guess there was a little problem in Philly when they tried to arrest VanDini. Apparently one of the Tony's was shot and killed in a shootout and the other one got away." LC had another call coming in so he told the Captain he would call him later. It was Jullio on the other line.

I've got some good news for you," the Philly attorney started out, "Everything went off without a hitch." LC then questioned him about the shootout. "Yea, Fat Tony Fabia shot it out with Philly's finest and lost and Tony, Matzo Balls Massini got away but we'll find him," Jullio stated. "No cops or innocent people were harmed and that's the main thing," he added.

Jullio also informed LC that Angelo VanDini was in custody and the Warden and Deputy Warden were under further investigation. "We have this latest plant on them which they don't know about and if we can get someone to talk or find more evidence in VanDini's safe then we'll slam them. I know that would make you very happy," Jullio sang the words that LC wanted to hear.

Jullio knew the whole sleazy story of the set up they tried on LC and so did the Judge and the Police Chief. He also knew it would be an easy case to win but he also knew it would never come to that. The Philadelphia lawyer always liked and respected LC. And when he saw how unglued he got over his honesty and integrity being questioned Jullio became a first hand witness of what a class act LC really was.

Now LC had another call coming in, it was Mike Zipp. Mike asked LC if he was with Kassaundra or had seen her. LC informed him that she had to get up early the day before cause she was flying to Nevada's capitol at 1PM. Mike told him she was scheduled to take part in the raid that morning. She was going to ride with him and Jackson and wasn't going to be told any details until they were well on their way to the Sander's house. Mike added that she was a no call, no show. "Maybe the brass screwed up and forgot to take her name off the work list," Mike stated but didn't sound like he meant it.

The next morning the Captain called LC again. He groggily looked at the clock, it read 7:15AM. Cimini asked him the same question Mike had asked the night before. Cimini apologized for waking him but she was not at roll call again and hadn't called off. LC informed the Captain about the flight to Carson City.

Captain Cimini then asked LC if he mentioned the raids or any part of the investigation to her. "Of course not," was LC's reply. "The only thing I can think of is that somehow she got wind of the police action about to take place either here or in Philly." The Captain continued, "She is originally from there and maybe she has some inside connections that tipped her off. Officer Johnson might have suspected that she to would be arrested and took off for parts unknown."

The Captain's voice softened and he spoke to LC for the first time as a concerned parent would to their child. "LC I know you have strong feelings for her and I feel terrible that she has probably skipped town, but you know I could not have informed her of the raids or even told her she would not be brought up on any charges. I just couldn't risk it. I told you in the beginning that I didn't want you harmed in anyway and I meant that. I didn't think I would be referring to a broken heart."

LC assured the Captain that he understood completely. "I'm a grown man," LC said, "The pain will fade with time but my memories of her will last forever." He knew that the finalization of this investigation might prove to be a tough nut to chew. Kassaundra would have to decide which side of the law she was on. She seemed like she was honestly upset for getting involved in this jewelry mess but LC figured she needed the money badly enough to take a chance of losing her job and messing up her life and career.

He would not harshly misjudge the girl because of one hasty mistake. Instead, he would judge her on the way she treated him and the many laughs and fun times they had shared. He had to admit to himself that there was a tugging on his heart that would not soon go away. LC found himself holding the bracelet he had bought for her and looking at the inscription. He would never, ever consider taking it back to Mel for re-imbursement. He would cherish it forever as he tried to remember the fragrance of her neck. LC blushed to himself because he could easily remember the softness of her skin and the firmness of her bosom.

CHAPTER 23
Postponed Love

I t had been two months and 21 days since the raids and the arrests that lead to this morning's court proceedings in the Clark County courthouse. The trial in Philadelphia, Pa. wouldn't start for another two or three months. Fortunately, cases weren't backed up as bad here in Sin City.

LC had already received close to $30,000.00 from Captain Cimini's bait money fund and there would be more to come once the Sander's material gains from criminal activity was cleared. He also received 10% of what he had coming from Philly Police Chief Power's program and that amounted to another $30,000.00. He was assured that a guilty verdict from VanDini's trial would bring him the balance of $270,000.00.

To make the desert sun even brighter LC was up $17,000.00 playing Blackjack, Caribbean Stud, Let-It-Ride and Texas Hold'em. His only problem in life right now was the hole in his heart left there by Kassaundra. The last time he went this long without a woman was when he was in the Army stationed at Fort Lewis, Washington for A.I.T. training. There were plenty of female volunteers back then, LC was a handsome younger man, but he refused to cheat on his second wife. LC vowed to himself that as soon as these trials were over he would get on with his love life. He would not allow himself to live in the past any longer.

LC had met with the lead prosecutor Marnie Parker. She was a scant five foot tall, cute as a button, but a real firebrand.

He wondered if she was married. She informed him that he would be the first witness called. After speaking with her for five minutes he actually felt sorry for Dave and Beverly Sanders.

As LC was walking to the stand to testify he heard a commotion in the back of the packed courtroom. He immediately recognized two old friends from his Correction days, Ed Loomis and John Griffith. They were supervisors also, although Ed had retired when LC did. He had to laugh as it appeared that the Griff-Dude had walked into the back of Ed-Bo. These were affectionate nick names LC had for them. He thought it only fair as they both called him Bubba. LC had no idea where they had got that from. Ed-Bo was about LC's size but the Griff-Dude was about 6'5" tall and 300 pounds. He chucked to himself again when he saw a wet spot on Ed-Bo's shirt. That told LC that the Griff-Dude had not changed. Whenever LC and the Griff-Dude would go out for drinks or to a restaurant he always managed to spill something on LC's clothes. He put up with this slight inconvenience because if anyone ever tried to pick a fight with LC for any reason Griff-Dude would grab him and lift his feet off the ground and politely explain to them that they were virtually on death's door if it ever happened again. They always got the message.

After being sworn in LC was asked by the prosecutor to inform the jury of his duties as a correctional supervisor, his subsequent retirement, his meetings and findings in Philadelphia and how he came to be in Las Vegas.

After the morning break he proceeded to tell the jury how he was approached by Captain Cimini through officers Zipp and Thomas and how he was offered the undercover job. He continued on the rest of the day relating to the jury their findings at the Sander's home.

The next day of his testimony LC explained to the panel of twelve how he met Angelo VanDini and the two Tonys. He went on about the offer VanDini made to him on the plane and how upon his return to Vegas he gave the parcel of fake or real diamonds to Angelo's daughter Beverly Sanders.

On day three he recalled to them the taped findings in the room behind the bar and that was placed into evidence as exhibit "A". He proceeded to relate to them all events leading up to the raids and the resulting evidence found at those addresses. At 4:30 he was allowed to step down. LC was cautioned not to speak to anyone of his testimony because he may be called to testify again.

The Judge announced that since the next witness was in the anterior room and had been waiting all day he would have her sworn in before adjourning for the day.

The bailiff rose, all 5'4" of him, and in his huskiest voice that still sounded like Michael Jackson's he called out, "The prosecution calls Kassaundra Henry."

LC had never heard of anyone named Kassaundra before and now there were two of them involved in the same case. He looked up just in time to see the girl he loved walk in from a side room. He of course knew her as Kassaundra Johnson but, after being sworn in, she announced her name as Kassaundra Henry. She then stated her occupation as an agent for the United States Department of Justice but presently working undercover as a Las Vegas Patrolman.

LC was sitting with officers Mike Zipp, Jackson Thomas and Captain Cimini, and all four had their jaws drop to their knees.

The judge then announced that the day's proceedings were over and court would re-adjourn at 9AM the next morning. Kassaundra was dismissed and before she departed out the same side door she had entered she placed her lips to her fingers, kissed them and tilted her head sideways. She then looked LC right in the eyes and blew him that kiss. No one else saw that demure little gesture but LC caught it. He immediately started to feel whole again.

LC knew he wouldn't be hearing from her that night and he fought the urge to call her. All this time he thought she had gotten caught up in this web of thievery because she had needed the money. Now it turns out she was receiving paychecks from two different agencies, as he was. He never knew for certain what side of the law she was on until about 4:30 that afternoon. She certainly surprised them all. LC wondered when Kassaundra had found out about him doing the undercover work and if she had been equally surprised. One thing for certain, they would have a good laugh when it was all over.

He had to meet his Philly friends, Ed and Griff again tonight. LC hoped he would have a chance to introduce Kassaundra to them before they had to fly home.

CHAPTER 24
Pandemonium

L C sat on one of the long benches in the hallway outside of Courtroom 3. He was supposed to meet his friends from the night before at breakfast. They never made it and LC figured out the likely reason. The Griff-Dude snores so loud, Ed-Bo probably hadn't slept in three days.

He looked at his watch; it was 8:45AM. LC would wait another ten minutes before going in to get a seat. He was excited about seeing Kassaundra and he reached inside his dress coat pocket to retrieve the tennis bracelet he had bought her. As LC traced his fingers over the diamond encrusted top his mind started to wonder. He shook his head from side to side to clear out the sensual thoughts that had suddenly charged in. He placed the bracelet back in the box and returned it to whence it came.

LC heard a clamor coming from the end of the hall near the restrooms. He knew who was making the fuss even before he looked up. Griff-Dude was trying to stifle his laughter and Ed-Bo was trying to cover up the wet spot on the front of his pants.

A third person walked out behind them and locked on to LC's gaze. Tony (Matzo Balls) Mancini was smiling at him and LC was smiling back. He wondered if Tony was an undercover agent also. The answer to that query was quickly realized when Tony pulled a pistol out of a potato chip bag. LC managed to make it to his feet just as Tony fired at him. The bullet hit him in the chest knocking him back against the bench and the wall behind it. Needless to say pandemonium followed.

LC's eyes and brain were working like a slow motion camera. The first thing he thought of was, "Wow that was a great shot!" Tony was at least 75 feet away.

LC was a good shot himself. He was top gun at the prison two years before his retirement, shooting a perfect 300 with the Glock and a 100 with the 12 gauge shotgun.

The next thing he saw was Ed-Bo taking Tony to the ground and the Griff-Dude disarming him. Griff then yanked him to his feet and slammed him against the wall. Tony was a big man but his feet were not touching the ground.

LC's mind wondered back ten years when he and Griff were exiting a local Philly tavern. The bouncer was kicking the shit out of some asshole up the street a little ways and there was a log jam at the door from the rubber neckers. Always the gentleman LC had said, "Excuse me," twice but one young buck was feeling his musk and wouldn't budge. LC gently moved him back just enough to get out but that apparently upset the lad. The foolish child then took a swing at the back of LC's head just as he was lighting a cigar. The Griff-Dude grabbed him with one hand and held him up against the wall, his feet suspended in the air. Griff was wagging his finger in his face and lecturing him like you would a child. That same scene was being played out again as Tony was in the grip of the gentle giant, frozen against the wall receiving his come up pence.

Just before he passed out LC watched the Sheriff's deputies ask Griff if they could handcuff Tony. They confiscated the gun Ed was standing on and they took Tony away.

LC felt a total peace come over his body. He remembered thinking he was probably dying. His thoughts were on

Kassaundra and her soft skin and tender lips. Then reality set in. Her soft skin needed a shave and her tender lips covered half his face. LC opened his eyes as the Griff-Dude was about to perform rescue breathing again. The word "again" is what brought LC back to life more than anything. "Get your big ass off me, I'm not Kathy," LC said referring to his lovely wife's name. The Griff-Dude stated proudly, "I was performing CRP." Ed was falling down with laughter as he corrected Griff, "That's CPR." Griff bellowed, "I was doing that to!"

LC told him, "You'll be performing in the circus as the one-nutted ogre if you don't get off me." Griff pulled him to his feet as the paramedics arrived.

LC was rubbing his chest and the back of his head but saw no blood on either hand. He felt like he had been struck with a golf ball. Hitting his head against the wall from the impact of the bullet is what had temporarily knocked him unconscious.

The one paramedic found a hole in LC's sport coat but not one in his shirt. LC reached into his coat pocket and pulled out the box with the bracelet. There was a nice round hole in the top of it but none on the bottom.

LC looked up and was surprised to see all his friends, new and old, surrounding him. The crowd parted quickly as if King Kong was coming through a corn field. LC was very glad to see a tearful Kassaundra rushing to his side rather than a large monkey.

"Oh my God, Oh my God, are you alright?" Kassaundra asked as tears ran down her cheeks. LC assured her that he was fine and then handed her the gift of love he had bought for her almost three months earlier. Kassaundra took off the lid and held it up to show the crowd the neat round hole. She then brushed aside the fancy paper and both looked closely at the top of the bracelet. One thing was certain, they were real diamonds and their reputation of being the hardest substance on earth was quickly proven.

Kassaundra picked up the bracelet and allowed the flattened slug to fall back into the box. She looked up and handed the box and contents to Captain Cimini who was directly behind LC as if it were planned. Her eyes were then transfixed on the inscription and they welled up with tears of joy this time.

Officer Jackson Thomas could hold back no longer, "LC, you have got to be the luckiest son-of-a-bitch on earth." LC's friends from Philly knew that he was not only referring to the close escape from death but also the fact that he was being doted on by a very lovely young woman.

Ed-Bo asked, "LC, How do you do it?" He and Griff knew what his answer would be as they had heard it many times over the years. "Clean living," LC replied, "If you live the straight and narrow life like I do, go things will happen to you also!" A collection of groans and laughter reverberated throughout the hallowed walls of the courthouse.

LC rebuffed the female medic who would have made Clara Barton proud at her persistence at trying to get LC to go to the hospital.

The bailiff "Squeaky Fromme" then announced that trial would re-convene in 5 minutes. Everything returned to normality and Kassaundra re-entered the courtroom to give her testimony.

LC and his friends from Vegas and Philly entered also. He felt a twinge of pain in his opposite shoulder as his good buddy and protector, the Griff-Dude walked him right into the door jamb. "Jesus Christ Griff," LC barked, "This friggin' doorway is six foot wide." The Griff-Dude didn't care, the lovable oaf was all smiles; his good friend was safe and sound.

CHAPTER 25
The Post Script

LC could hardly wait for Kassaundra to get home from work to tell her the good news. Her initial intentions were to resign from the Justice Department and accept the position Captain Cimini had offered her as a detective sergeant for the Las Vegas Police Department. But the United States Department of Justice did not want to lose an officer with her experience and expertise so they put her second in charge of the Las Vegas office.

The good news he had for her she knew nothing about. The Justice Department accepted the bid LC had offered for the Sander's residence that they had confiscated. He had picked it up for a fraction of its assessed value.

The happy fairy had finally landed on LC's shoulder and life was good. Two months earlier LC received the balance of the $300,000 from Philadelphia. He got an additional $22,000 from Captain Cimini. He was still winning at the gambling tables and Kassaundra was living with him and their relationship had blossomed even more. And to put more icing on the cake, he had gotten word that one of his ex-bosses at Graterford was somebody's bitch in the prison where they both ended up in.

Two days earlier he received a phone call that there may be a possible book and movie deal in the works about parts of his life and the results of his undercover job.

Who the hell would want to buy a book about Lassiter Carson?